A Glimpse of the Rainbow

PHILOMENA VAN OORT

WESTBOW
P R E S S®
A DIVISION OF THOMAS NELSON
& ZONDERVAN

This is a work of fiction. All of the characters, names, incidents, organizations, and dialogue in this novel are either the products of the author's imagination or are used fictitiously.

WestBow Press books may be ordered through booksellers or by contacting:

WestBow Press
A Division of Thomas Nelson & Zondervan
1663 Liberty Drive
Bloomington, IN 47403
www.westbowpress.com
1 (866) 928-1240

Scripture taken from the King James Version of the Bible.

ISBN: 978-1-9736-7134-3 (sc)
ISBN: 978-1-9736-7135-0 (hc)
ISBN: 978-1-9736-7133-6 (e)

Library of Congress Control Number: 2019911027

Print information available on the last page.

WestBow Press rev. date: 08/27/2019

Dedicated with honor to

The Creator who sacrificed His only Son,
The One who sent Himself as a ransom for many.
May this book bring Thee honor and glory.

My precious Dad, thank you, thank you, thank you
For all your perpetual support and unconditional love;
I truly could never be the writer I am today without you.

My dear Mother who carried me for nine months,
Thank you for your enduring love and devotion,
And for helping me become the young woman God intended.

My dear siblings, Colton & Evangeline, my nephew, Wesley,
Heather, Savannah, Christianna, and Robert Jr.
I love you all to the ends of the earth!

My dear cousins with whom I shared my youth.
Maren, Christen, Silas, and Nathaniel,
Cheers to all our special childhood memories!

Elise Stephanson,
Thank you for believing in my dream.
God bless you in life's beautiful journey.

Contents

"And this is the promise that he hath promised us, even eternal life."

1 John 2:25

Prologue

May, 1884

London, England

Annette Davison sat upon a chair overlooking the sea. It was a Sunday afternoon. Despite how exhausted the woman was, she had put up a brave front by deliberately enjoying precious moments with her daughter.

Five year old Elizabeth ran along the shore, squealing in delight as water gushed up from behind a rock to spray her each time a wave rolled in. Annette smiled. It did the little girl real good to play this way.

The mother's joy then evaporated as she gazed out over the water. Life was definitely difficult for her, but Annette Davison specifically chose to focus on the little things and not just the big things. Her motto was to 'Enjoy her life to the fullest'. The woman gave a wry smile that did not hide the emptiness she felt. Ah, yes. That was partially true. She did enjoy nature to the fullest. But it was still only nature. It did not have the same sensibilities as her life. No, she decided, it did not reflect her life. Her life was bleak, dark and cold.

The young mother's smile broadened when she heard her daughter shriek again. The tide had reached the young girl and had dragged part of her dress under the water. Elizabeth grabbed a handful of sand and threw it out into the waves. The result was so captivating that she once again picked up a handful of sand and threw it into the sea, this time pausing to gaze deeply into the depths to determine where the tiny grains of sand had disappeared to.

Annette continued to gaze out over the water, absorbing the beauty of the elements. She was dazzled by the creative beauty of God in the most overwhelming vision before her. It seemed to stretch on forever ahead before and beyond her. The azure blue of the elements seemed to stretch out until it reached and blended into the firmament. They consorted together until they blended as one to form a single nearly indiscernible line as far as the eye could see. Waves continued to crash against the shore while a deep rumble of thunder echoed repeatedly from above. Annette glanced up quickly, debating whether to call Elizabeth and head back to their cottage. Upon seeing her daughter's face, she decided against it. Let it rain, she thought. Let it pour. She would stay to relish the refreshing moment. It wasn't often that they went to the shore together, and it certainly was not very often that she could see her daughter this contented.

The sky darkened abruptly just before the first few raindrops sprinkled down. Elizabeth spread her hands over her head and made a quick leap nearly completing a three hundred and sixty degree turn before her giddy euphoria erupted into a beautiful, carefree girlish delight.

Annette watched her daughter run along the shoreline, pausing at times to kick the sand beneath her feet. It was some time before the little girl tired, but eventually she made her way up to where her mother sat and climbed dolefully up into her mother's arms. She laid her auburn head against her mother's shoulder and neither of them spoke a word for a few minutes. Annette held her daughter, resting her chin upon the damp hair. She relished in the moment, enjoying her daughters childhood.

It was Elizabeth that finally spoke, breaking the silence of the moment by expressing her delight in the opportunity to play near the water. She never did seem to be able to keep quiet much longer than a minute.

Annette closed her eyes to blink away a few tears. Her little girl was growing up so fast. Oh, how she wished to keep her young daughter in her arms forever. Just to keep her close forever!

Don't be selfish, she upbraided herself sternly. *She is going to grow up soon and become a young woman so beautiful that I won't even recognize her in a few years!* Despite how hard the woman tried to push away her own selfish thoughts, however, another nostalgic tear trickled down her cheek. *Stop crying. You are just feeling sorry for yourself.*

But she couldn't stop. She just had to cry for the little girl in her arms. She had to cry for her little girl who would so soon no longer *be* her little girl.

Elizabeth happened to tilt her head up and, observing her mother's tear stained face, a look of horror crossed her young, delicate features. "Mama!" she exclaimed, aghast. "Why are you crying?"

Annette shook her head, wildly attempting to rub away the evidence of tell-tale tears. "Oh no, darling, I'm not crying," she lied. "They are only raindrops, you see? They just make me look like I am crying."

Oh, God, forgive my lie, she begged. *But I cannot let my little girl take on any more of life's burdens than she has already! She must remain innocent to life's hateful sneering face. I must protect her from the ravages that life appears to have already planned for her the moment she arrived into this troublesome world.*

Elizabeth did not appear to believe her mother's words. She frowned. "But I don't have any raindrops on my face!" she exclaimed indignantly.

Annette laughed. A laugh that was filled with painful reality. Elizabeth was growing up too fast for her own good.

"You are *covered* in droplets," she teased. "But not really from the raindrops. It is from the water when it crashed against the shoreline."

The girl nodded. "Oh," she said, before she turned the conversation to talk a mile a minute on another of her unrealistic fantasies.

Annette listened somewhat absentmindedly while, closing her eyes dreamily. She so loved her child. Her beautiful daughter.

"Mama." The little girl broke into her mother's thoughts again.

She jerked awake. She had almost been sleeping she realized with a start. Her eyes snapped open and she turned to gaze resolutely into Elizabeth's sea-green eyes. "Yes, my darling?"

The child smiled a smile that beamed like crystals even as the sinking sun shone upon her cherry red lips. "Look," she repeated breathlessly. "A rainbow over the water!"

Annette followed Elizabeth's outstretched arm and dimpled finger until she too saw the rainbow. She drew a sharp intake of breath. The rainbow followed the walls of the firmament in a beautiful arch shape. Its colors were of such brilliance they were nearly hypnotizing.

Elizabeth's gaze was transfixed. She gazed upwards in absolute awe and wonder. "Mama," she began. "Where does the end of the rainbow go?"

Annette turned shocked eyes upon her daughter. "Whatever do you mean, Elizabeth?" she asked, puzzled.

The little girl tipped her head in the cutest gesture ever imagined. "Well, the rainbow touches the water and then it ends. Where is the end of the rainbow?"

Annette paused to digest her daughter's strange yet intriguing question. "I...I guess I've never really thought about that." The women furrowed her brow. Sometimes the questions her daughter came up with really made her think.

"Or is there an end somewhere where we can't see it?" persisted the young girl.

A faraway look came to Annette's eyes. She smiled as though she knew the secret. "Did you know that beyond each rainbow is a pot of gold? Oh yes, a beautiful pot of gold that shimmers and shines and glimmers in the beaming sunlight. Many people have heard about the pot of gold and have ventured to search for it, but it is a very, very difficult thing to find. There is a profusion of obstacles that detain many a person who sets out to reach this hidden treasure. Some people being often obstructed by mishaps and such, turn around and set back for home. Then there are others who nearly reach the gold pot. However, just before they find it, some other discouragement encompasses their way, and they become so despondent and frustrated that they turn around and return in the way they came. Again, there are still others who are persistent and place their faith in God alone, the One who sees everything upon the face of the earth, and attached a real message of promise to the rainbow."

Elizabeth appeared rather overwhelmed and awed by her mother's words. Her mouth had dropped slightly with wonder. "Satisfied?" Annette Davison tweaked her daughter's upturned, lightly freckled nose, which brought forth another smile to her daughters face. Just that quickly, the child frowned and it appeared that she was thinking deeply.

"What else, Mama?"

"What else? Well, those who really believe that Jesus is with them every step of the way find the treasure. And I will say from experience that they who have found it have found the true meaning of life."

Elizabeth leaned her head back against her mother's shoulder. "Is that all? There is no money or rich things?"

Annette smiled at her daughter's pensive expression. "What is 'all' is *everything!* Being rich isn't everything. Sometimes it is better to be poor and happy. Like I am."

Annette *was* happy. Yet the bitterness she felt towards life was nearly too much to bear at times. She struggled hard each day against all the hardships and confusion. She often wished that she were still that cheerful, lively little girl from many years ago. Regardless of how much she yearned for something different, life remained the same. Each new day was the same as the last…at least to her, anyways. But of course she was happy. She had God in her heart and Elizabeth in her life!

Yet she was not entirely happy. If only life would mean something other than just living and breathing and working each day. If only it meant some enjoyment. But to Annette it did not. She thought it dreary and empty. She had discovered that her thoughts of Life often betrayed her. You thought it was on your side until it would backlash, retaliating its so-called friendship, striking you down. Oh, how she knew that so well. Her own life had so often been filled with unexpected turns and disappointments.

Elizabeth was speaking yet again, her tone of voice very clear and pronounced. As always, she was speaking her mind. "Well, I would prefer to be rich rather than poor. Being poor is not nice. You do not get all the nice things that rich people do."

The woman's heart sank at her daughter's words. Her response was sharp. The unpleasant results of her own past were laced between her words. She was afraid her daughter would make the same mistake she had. She wanted to ensure that her daughter would never confide in others the personal griefs and disappointments of life's journey that she might experience. Oh, how she prayed Elizabeth would stand strong upon her own two feet and would never consent to trusting in anyone but the Lord Himself.

"Life will seem to befriend you, and then quite unexpectedly, you will find yourself betrayed by its allurements and promises. When you experience disappointments, do not be swallowed up by them, but overcome them through faith. Do not make the same mistake I did. Trust in no one except God. He will never forsake you." The woman closed her eyes. "Oh, Elizabeth. Please do not ever become the person who claims there is no such thing as a rainbow's pot of gold. How I pity them! They don't know what they are missing! You must continue searching for the rainbow's pot of gold. If you never forsake trusting in the Lord, you will reach the end of the rainbow."

Again, Elizabeth did not fully understand the deeper meaning of her mother's words, but unbeknown to her, her mother's message subconsciously sank into her memory. Many years later she would experience and savor her mother's words.

Chapter One

Tears trickled down pale cheeks. "Mama, I need you here. Why did you have to go?"

The slender eight-year-old buried her face in the blanket, smudging the silver lines on her cheeks. A sudden knock on their small cottage door had her sitting up straight.

"Wh-who is there?" she dared to venture, green eyes as round as marbles. There was no reply. The knocking persisted, unrelenting.

Fear struck her heart before the young girl put her head back down into the folded corner of the soft blankets and wept. Her mother was gone; she was alone. She just wanted to die!

———

Noah Charles Harrison, the right and honorable lord of Blivington Castle, sighed impatiently. Why wasn't anyone answering the door? And where was his indentured servant, Annette?

He reflected on the time when he had first met Annette as though it had only occurred yesterday. Noah had happened upon the woman in a most unlikely manner while on his voyage from Scotland back to England.

Memories of the frightened woman flooded his mind.

1

———

1878
Edinburgh, Scotland

He saw the fear that shadowed her and the way she looked around, over her shoulder and behind her. She was afraid of something.

Noah Harrison watched her for a few moments, trying to discern what type of woman she was. What was she doing here by the ship's dock? She looked respectable, he concluded, so she must be from the middle class.

She was attired in a dark brown dress and a starched white apron fitted snugly around her small waist. A deep burgundy cloak hung loosely over her shoulders. She had a look of pride and dignity about her that made a person look her way again.

Pretty couldn't begin to describe her looks. With strawberry blonde hair and blue-green eyes, her facial features were vivacious. Curls bounced about her face. She must have noticed his eyes upon her for she turned, appraising him silently, her eyes piercing his. If she had hoped for him to appear disconcerted, she was mistaken. He remained where he was, eyes fixed upon her.

She studied him surreptitiously for a few more moments. It seemed as though she was eyeing him with a look of defiance, almost daring him to make a move. Her stance was rigid, and her spine as straight as a pin.

To his surprise, she approached him.

"Miss," Noah said gently. "May I help you with anything?"

Her expression tensed. "I ask for nothing, except that I absolutely *must* go to England."

"You want to go to England?" Noah repeated slowly.

The young woman frowned. "No, sir! I *must* go to England. England is my destiny."

Noah quirked an eyebrow. "Why? Why would a young woman

such as yourself have to go to England? Are you running away from something? Are you in trouble with the law or…a man?"

The woman's eyes flashed. "I am not asking any questions of you nor of what your business is here. It isn't any of your concern."

"I beg your pardon?" The lord frowned disapprovingly at her disrespectful response.

"It is the truth, sir!" she exclaimed forcefully. "Is there a reason you are asking such questions, or is it only idle curiosity?"

Noah Harrison gaped openly at her blunt retort. She was very outspoken and not at all hesitant to speak her mind. But didn't she realize whom she was talking to? Didn't she know that she was talking to a lord and that it was within his rights to have her put into prison for disrespectful words or actions against him?

"Do you realize who I am?" he questioned almost threateningly.

She glared at him, defiance written all over her features. "Yes, sir, I do. You are a self-centered man. And it is the pure truth of it, too!"

He gawked. Never before had he met a woman so outspoken! But didn't she understand that her quick-witted, quick-to-answer tongue could soon cost her freedom?

"Allow me to warn you that if I were a man of lesser character, I would've already thrown you into prison for how you are speaking to me."

To his surprise, glistening tears filled her luminous eyes. Compassion stole over his soul. "Pray tell, why are you crying?"

She only shook her head dolefully. "This country is a land filled with hate and greed. The men who rule this land have allowed people to raise themselves up and to have the power to take anything they can from anyone of lesser means in money or heritage. The rich prey upon the poor as an eagle preys upon a mouse. They think only of themselves!" She glanced up at him, her eyes filling with sadness. "But please do not believe I am an imbecile." She straightened her shoulders. "If I have insulted you in any event, I apologize. I plead for you to not get me into trouble with the authorities. I-I just forgot myself…and my place."

Noah contemplated her for a moment. "I forgive you for how you affronted me. However, I am not the type of person who 'preys' upon people of a lesser class." He hesitated. "The words you spoke regarding our countries…no doubt you are speaking from your own experiences. You are talking about how you have been affected by its greed. What stories are you hiding in your heart?"

She jerked back as though he had stung her like a bee. "I am hiding nothing at all," she snapped.

He raised his eyebrows in disbelief. "As you say."

She softened slightly. "I am unable to disclose my business to you. It is ineffective to tell anyone." He opened his mouth to respond, but she continued relentlessly. "You can't understand what I am saying as you have never been where I am! Maybe you think that if I were to tell you, you could understand and then assist me in my predicament, but the only thing you could help me with is to get to across to England! Other than that, only God can help me."

Her words were tinted with fear, and her voice shook. The panic in her eyes was partially hidden by a look of consternation as she glanced about nervously once more. Perhaps she was being followed by some shifty character. Or perhaps she'd been kidnapped and had just managed to escape. Could that be why she was asking to go to England? Because she wanted to escape the life she had always known and begin anew?

"Miss, I assure you that I will not pressure you to reveal your secret to me."

Her eyes brightened slightly. "Oh sir, if only you could help me by recompensing my passage to England. I will pay you back every cent. On my word of honor, I will! But I currently do not have any money."

"May I ask your name?"

"Yes, sir. It is Annette." She paused. "Annette MacEwan."

Noah said nothing about her obvious hesitation regarding her name. "All right, Miss MacEwan. I will pay your passage to England

4

and give you a place to live if you agree to work at my estate as an indentured servant for fifteen years."

A smile broke out upon her lips. "I thank you from the bottom of my heart, sir. I accept your offer with the deepest gratitude I own, and I promise I will work hard for you."

He knew he had done the right thing. "I see the ship is preparing her leave. Shall we go aboard?"

Her teary smile beamed the rays of a rainbow, and he knew he had his answer.

————

Bringing his thoughts back to the present, Noah exhaled a breath, rubbing his hands together to ward off the cold.

And that was how Annette MacEwan now Annette Davison had become his indentured servant. She had worked for him over eight years now.

What an addition she had made when she'd first entered the castle. The other servants had all been surprised by her outspokenness. She said words that most would shrink from even daring to think. She met every person's eyes unflinchingly. She challenged them silently, unafraid. Her eyes stole a deeper look into their souls, something that made a person of lesser character cringe, while those of honest heart would wish to begin a friendship.

He wondered how she had fared during his absence. It had been nearly two years ago that Noah Harrison had left England. The tall lord had been away to a coastal village through the doctor's recommendation. If he would have continued living in England, he could have been susceptible to some potentially deadly illness.

Noah contemplated Annette's life shortly after she'd arrived into England.

About only a month after they had returned to England, the young woman announced to have fallen in love with the stable hand who claimed to have feelings for her in return. And so it was only shortly after that they were married. A few months later she'd begun to show with child. It had been one blustery autumn evening that a feisty little girl arrived into the hardships of life she would soon realize existed. The proud parents named the child Elizabeth Hannah Davison.

Elizabeth Davison's complexion was absolutely that of a redhead's. Vivacious green eyes, a pert little nose and a heart shaped face; she was a girl that stood out in a crowd with the smattering of freckles dusting her cheeks and nose.

The ghost of a smile upon his features curved upwards. Ah, the child would be nigh on eight years old by now, and never a day had passed that Noah Harrison had not thought about the girl. The spirit of determination and strength within her...oh, he loved Elizabeth as though she were his own daughter. She was the one who brought him laughter in his old age. She was the one who sang him the familiar Scottish songs taught by her mother in her cute lisp. She was the one who reacted to situations in a most remarkable and entirely amusing manner. She was the second most important person in his life, next to his son, of course. How he had missed her these two long years.

Bringing his thoughts back to the present, Noah felt the cold creep into his bones. The snow swirled around him, stinging his face, and he could feel the north wind through his thick coat.

He frowned. Behind the closed door in front of him, the lord thought he heard someone weeping. Curiosity got the better of him, and he pressed his ear against the door. Indeed, there was someone crying inside. Something was wrong.

He tried the door and found it unlocked. Opening it hesitantly, he slowly entered. Softly closing the door behind himself, he turned to see the familiar table, two chairs, a small dingy window, and a small cooking stove. Although the cottage was cold and dark, he could still distinguish a door going into the back room.

"Is there anyone home?" he asked the now silent house.

The bedroom door suddenly squeaked as it slowly began to open. A small girl entered the main room.

He stared at her in surprise.

She sniffed. "Mr. Harrison!"

Was this Elizabeth? His pulse quickened. Yes, it was the dear child. How it did his heart good to see the young girl again.

Her lower lip quivered despite her strong resolve to hold back the tears. "My mama died."

His heartwarming thoughts were suddenly showered with dismay. Had he heard right?

"I beg your pardon?"

Tears sprang to the child's eyes. "Mama is...is dead. At least I am very certain she has passed away."

His eyes reflected sorrow. "I offer my condolences." He hesitated. "Could I perhaps see your mother, my dear?"

The girl nodded tentatively. "Yes, sir."

Noah followed her as she led him towards the dingy room where she'd first seen him. In the corner of the room there lay a cot. On it, Noah saw, was the form of a woman. He could scarcely believe his eyes. It was Annette! But it was not the same Annette Davison he had left a few years ago. She looked like a different woman.

Oh, how old and frail she seemed! Under her eyes were dark blue lines and her cheeks appeared pale and hollow. He cleared his throat. There was no response. When she didn't move, Noah stepped forwards and lifted the limp, white hand. It was cold. He felt for the pulse, but there was none. Gently putting the hand back down, he turned back towards Beth. Her eyes betrayed hope. But when she saw his grave look she knew that her mother really was dead.

He watched her swallow hard as she turned and then led the way towards the front door. Noah slowly followed her. He knew he couldn't allow the child to stay here. Not in the cold house and all by herself. He decided to take her along to the castle. At least she would be with people who would care for her.

"Beth?" The child looked at him. He drew a deep, deep breath.

"I think you should come to the castle with me tonight. I would be concerned for you alone here. It would be not safe."

The child's eyes brightened exceedingly despite the sad pain that filled the green eyes. Even though they glistened from unshed tears, he saw a sparkle fill them. "Only if it wouldn't be too much trouble, sir," she answered. He just smiled when she placed her small hand into his large one. And after pulling the door shut behind them, they disappeared into the blustery world of white that swallowed them up like a blizzard.

Chapter Two

Nine-year-old Elizabeth sat beside her mother's grave. Tears slid down her pale cheeks. "Oh, Mama, that awful person. Today he put a frog in my slipper and I stepped on it. I nearly *killed* him, Mama! That dreadfully cruel and mean boy just stood there laughing so hard he actually fell onto the ground into fits of convulsive laughter. He was laughing…at me! Oh, I just hate him."

She clenched her little teeth and fists together to better accommodate her fury towards the boy.

The pale blue sky did not reflect her feelings at all. Neither did the orange, red and yellow leaves that scattered the well-worn path. Elizabeth slowly rose and made her way back towards the castle, her shoulders slouched and her features drawn into a forlorn frown.

————

1893

Elizabeth Hannah Davison lifted her auburn hair off her flushed face, tucking a silken strand behind her ear. She sighed as she dipped her hard-bristled brush back into the bucket of water and then scrubbed the floor again.

Six years ago her mother had passed away from the tragic illness

9

of Tuberculous. A few months ago, Noah Harrison had decided that she was to begin working. This was the first year that counted off the debt still owed by Annette Davison. The poor woman had passed away, leaving the remaining eight years of indentured service to be completed by her daughter, Elizabeth.

The tingling memories of her mother often flooded the surface of the girl's mind. Oh, she did not mind to work in the stead of her mother. She did not mind to scrub floors or wash dishes. She did not mind to peel potatoes or help prepare meals. In fact, she felt obliged to do it in return for all the generosity Noah Harrison had bestowed upon her. But it was the rage that accosted her whenever her thoughts turned to that wretched David Harrison. She was certain the boy gloated that she had to work like all the other children on the estate. If she closed her eyes tightly, she could just see him standing before her, proud, lofty, and cynical.

Unfortunately, David was the next heir to the castle. And with his father having recently fallen ill, her future did not look extremely bright. When Noah Harrison passed away, David Harrison would naturally take his position as rightful heir to the castle and its grounds! The young girl shivered at the thought of having to work for that ne'er-do-well.

"Are you still doing this floor?"

The brush clattered across the floor and her elbow bumped into the tin pail at her side, causing the bucket to tip precariously as the sudsy water sloshed dangerously from side to side.

Elizabeth jerked out of her deep ponderings and whirled around, face ashen. A ridiculously tall figure stood directly behind her in the doorway. Arrogance was the first word that came to mind as their eyes met. One shoulder leaned against the doorframe, his feet crossed at the ankles, while he folded his arms across his chest, quirking a brow. She supposed some would call him handsome although she refused to acknowledge it herself. She was daily surrounded by tittering, blushing maids who behaved very foolishly whenever they saw him. They chattered as jaybirds all throughout the day about that slothful, self-conceited bloke, each competing with each other, gossiping about each other, and spreading falsehoods about each other. It was enough to make her cast up her accounts. Besides, in Elizabeth's opinion, any person, whether that be a man, woman, or child who conducted themselves in such an egoistic, arrogant, prideful manner, deserved nothing but repulsion.

And David Harrison was prime example of that.

Eyes that were bluer than the mesmerizing crystalline water of the sea blazed across the room. She narrowed her eyes at the arrogant tightening that stretched along his straight, strong jaw line. He had tousled black hair that was thick and lustrous, reaching the back of his neck. His nose was strong and defined, his features molded from granite. A broad forehead only appeared to enhance his thick dark eyebrows that, although usually sloping downwards in a serious expression, were now raised as though he were mocking her. A lock of his wavy hair had slipped down across his forehead, making him look most exasperatingly infernal. He was well north of six feet, something that made irritation surge through her whenever she tried to stand him down with her own five foot, six inches. She hated it when he used his height to intimidate her.

Not that it did, of course. Well, she grudgingly amended, maybe a little bit.

That wretched boy, David Harrison. Oh, that horrible clodhopping galoot.

Her expression remained dull and placid although her words were laced with an artificial sugar coating that so obviously mocked any 'respect' she may have been ordered to use while speaking with '*his lordship*'.

"Begging your pardon, *Mr.* Harrison, but is it really necessary to frighten one when they are dutifully working? I nearly spilled the bucket of water upon my clean floor as a result of you not alerting me to your *wonderful* presence."

A smile curved his lips and it looked as though he were amused. She fervently hoped he was not.

"Is that so? Well, thank you for telling me. As you suggested, I certainly shall endeavor to prevent any 'incident' from occurring again in the future. But about nearly spilling the bucket of water on the floor…" He shook his head and frowned slightly. "I have been standing here for about ten minutes and not once have I seen you brush that floor. I do believe that you were in deep thought and not within the reality of your duties. Am I correct?"

Elizabeth knew that he was only making fun of her. Just because he was six years older than her did not mean he could treat her like a little street urchin!

She gritted her teeth. "I am well aware of the situation I am in, Mr. Harrison. And yes, sir, I admit to have been a world away. Please accept my apology and excuse me. I shall endeavor to remain focused on my present assignment."

The tall man analyzed her defiant expression beneath her pleasant facade. "Apology accepted. Have a good day, Beth."

Elizabeth fumed silently as he pushed his overbearing body away from the doorframe and turned away from her. Anger spilled through her veins. If only that slothful David Harrison had never been born! The wretched louse. He was so superior that it made her want to vomit. Perhaps the next time he came upon her, she would attack him. The question was, would she triumph in a fight? The girl doubted it although she was aware that one never knew until they tried. She bit her lip, considering the option to defeating him physically. After all, what other alternatives were there? Verbally, she never seemed to succeed as he always had answers that left her stumped and lorded his position over her. And mentally, she screamed words of hate at him. However, as they were within her mind, he was unable to hear them.

The girl expelled another breath of frustration. If she *were* to attack David Harrison, and if she *were* able to succeed, how could she face Noah Harrison?

"I am dreadfully sorry, sir, but I just killed your son because he aggravated me again. I was unable to take it anymore. Thus, I attacked him, and although he put up a good fight, the result was… death. Would you consider allowing me to perform the funeral? I could chant 'Hallelujah! that good-for-nothing lazybones is dead!' the entire ceremony."

Elizabeth scoffed. Utterly ridiculous. That would never work. No. There was only one recourse and that was to withstand the irritation that cursed boy imposed upon her.

———

North West Territories, Canada

Lemuel Ellis Keagan expelled a deep sigh.

His breath came out in a cloud of mist in the deepening fog. It was dusk. The wailing howl of a lone wolf brought a sense of peacefulness to the elderly man, and he inhaled deeply, relishing the beauty nature provided.

His thoughts could not help but turn to his beautiful Olivia. She had been so full of spunk and so filled with determination. But now that was all over. The perseverance and the persistence was gone in a cold grave. Everything he had loved and admired about her was gone.

Only memories.

He closed his eyes, wishing to relieve the sadness the reminiscence brought.

———

"Papa." The soft voice sounded immensely worried. "Papa, Rankin has not yet returned."

Lemuel looked up at his beautiful grown up daughter. "What's wrong, Livie?" he questioned.

"Rankin went fishing early this morning. He left a note saying he would return a little after dawn, just in time for breakfast. I am quite anxious as he still hasn't arrived, and it's now past dinnertime. Could you perhaps…?"

"Sweetheart, I'll go out and look for him," Lemuel interrupted, resting a gentle hand upon her shoulder.

She clasped her hands together. "Oh, thank you!"

Lemuel smiled. It was hard to refuse any request his daughter asked. "I'll be back with Rankin afore you even knew I'd been gone," he teased, and she smiled.

"I love you, Papa."

"I love you too. I'll be back soon."

"With Rankin." Her dreamy brown eyes held hope and devotion in them, making it easy to see that his daughter loved her husband immensely.

"With Rankin," Lemuel confirmed, smiling slightly at her pensive expression.

But he never did return with Olivia's husband. Lemuel found the river vacated and quiet. On the bank, there were footprints skidding down into the half-frozen waters. It was then that he suspected the poor man had slipped, falling under the water and beneath the ice.

Rationally, he knew there wasn't any hope in saving Rankin. Sadness filled his heart as he thought about his poor son-in-law. However, his heart became even more leaden as he thought about Olivia. How would she respond to the dreadful news that her husband had died?

Dreading the arrival back at the small shanty, Lemuel shuffled through the cold woods, taking as long as he possibly could. When he opened the small cabin door he was met by his daughter's beaming, enthusiastic face.

"I already have the biscuits on and I even made a special dessert for us four." She stated, running her fingers through her young son's hair. "Its blueberry pie the blueberries I collected and picked last summer. I even used some sugar that Rankin bought me for my birthday last fall!" Her face took on a radiant glow. "And when I fry Rankin's fish " She frowned slightly. "Where is Rankin?"

Peering around Lemuel's shoulders, the young woman looked about anxiously for her husband. Puzzled, she turned and looked up at her father's grave face. "P-Papa?" she asked, her chin trembling a little.

"Livie, sweetheart, I'm sorry. I found Rankin's footprints down by the river. He slipped and must have fallen in under the ice…" Lemuel watched her shake her head profusely before she began to cry. "Olivia, I'm so sorry," he said again, feeling helpless.

"No!" she cried. "No, it just can't be. It can't be true. You must be mistaken!" But even as she spoke the words, she knew that it was the truth and that her father was not mistaken.

Lemuel drew her into his arms and let her cry. He felt his own tears mingle with hers. He'd never seen his daughter so distressed and it hurt him. "Please…don't cry."

The young woman shook her head, moving out of his arms. More tears streamed down her cheeks. " 'Don't cry?' " she burst out, clearly hysterical. "You expect me not to cry when I hear that my beloved is dead? How will I live without him?"

Nearly the entire evening Lemuel sat beside her holding her cold hand. He only left once to tuck his grandson in bed. Olivia was cold but she couldn't even shiver. She merely sat in a chair staring ahead stoically, tears spilling over her cheeks.

Lemuel turned as soft padded footsteps entered the room. A little boy stood there, rubbing the sleep from his eyes. The elderly man gestured the boy over. After scooping the lad upon his knee, the boy leaned back and allowed his grandpa's secure arms to hold him. Lemuel rested his head against the wall and dozed off, forgetting to watch Olivia.

He was dead tired.

Chapter Three

London, England

"Where are you?" Elizabeth screamed, tears sliding down her cheeks. Where was David? She ran outside into the courtyard.

Nobody.

She followed the well-worn path that ran into the woods where her mother's grave was located.

No one was in sight.

Sobbing, she stumbled over a log and fell, ripping the hem of her dress. She struggled to rise and continue her search but then stumbled once more. Her ankle twisted in a hole. She gritted her teeth together to better compensate the agony.

She tried to stand, but the agony was too immense to bear. Looking up at the darkening sky, the girl felt waves of dread crash through her heart. Her ankle stung stabbing spasms of pain so violently that she had to clamp her teeth down on her lower lip to retain the sobs from escaping her throat.

The afternoon was fading fast. It was nigh on dusk now. What if she had to spend the night out here all alone? What if a predator might creep up on her unannounced and attack her innocent self?

She had heard from the gardeners that there were wolves around the castle grounds. Panic seeped in and along with it came self-pity.

This is all David's fault, she thought bitterly. *If he hadn't wandered so far from the castle, I wouldn't have twisted my ankle. It's his entire fault!*

Glancing down at her ankle, she attempted to gauge how bad her ankle really was. Gingerly she reached out her hand and touched it. Another scorching stab of pain zipped through her being. She bit back the sobs.

Her ankle was swelling rapidly. Was it sprained or perhaps even broken?

Suddenly pair of feet were in front of her. Confused, she looked up.

David Harrison stood there before her, amusement etched on his strong, chiseled features. Elizabeth's confusion transformed into raw fury. "Where have you been? I was looking everywhere."

In her frustration, she appeared to have forgotten that she was talking to her lord's son. She just spat out everything she thought... which was the real Elizabeth. She had been taught to be more subdued than impulsive, but now she forgot all the rules her mother had drummed into her mind. The girl spoke what she thought, not considering that she might be in major trouble with Mr. Harrison for how she was speaking to his son.

But that wretched boy didn't answer. He just looked down at her, contemplating her. Seeing her for who she really was.

She squirmed under his steady appraisal, and then repeated her question. "Where were you?"

Then he spoke in his most irritating voice. She was certain he was just using his horrible monotone tone just to make her upset.

"What happened to you, Beth? You look awfully messy. And apparently you slipped..." He eyed her awkwardly twisted leg.

Elizabeth closed her eyes, trying to relieve the pain. "I know. It was just that I was running, and then I tripped over a log. And as I attempted to regain my balance, my ankle tumbled in a hole." Pain spiraled through her, and she bit her bottom lip to suppress the ready tears. It wouldn't do any good to appear as a sniveling female in front of him. But, oh, how her foot hurt!

She burst into tears as another sharp searing pain shot through her ankle.

"Beth, why are you crying? What's wrong?" When she didn't answer, he raised his voice. "What's wrong? I demand you tell me at once!"

Elizabeth stuttered. His words were harsh and demanding. Anger flooded her. How dare he speak to her in such a tone?

Again the tall young man spoke. "Answer me. I must know what you are crying about." His tone had softened slightly. It was still persistent but it had alleviated some, making her feel more at ease.

Elizabeth licked her dry lips. "It's your father. He…uh…he wants you now."

David tensed instantly. "Are you implying that my father…" His voice trailed off as he thought about what he was about to say. "Do you mean he is worsening?"

Elizabeth sniffed back tears, suddenly becoming aware to whom she was speaking. Her tone of voice became subdued. "No, I mean, yes, Mr. Harrison."

David's face grew near ashen. "You mean he is nearly…?"

Elizabeth nodded. "Yes, sir. And I am so sorry Dav Mr. Harris"

"David, Beth. My name is David." He frowned, anxiety seeping his features. "My father is requesting my presence?"

The girl nodded, tears now freely sliding down her cheeks. "I advise you to hasten to his chamber. I've been searching for you for at least a half hour. I only hope I am not too late…" She sniffed back a tear and swallowed hard.

He nodded, but then shook his head. "What about you? Did you sprain your ankle?"

"I'll be fine. Please, just go to him!" Her voice quavered most exasperatingly.

Oh, why wouldn't that stupid boy go? Mr. Harrison senior was dying…probably dead by now! But David just stood there, torn between his ailing father and the injured girl at his feet. He couldn't leave her all alone here. He wasn't as heartless as she thought he was.

"I can't just leave you here all alone," he protested. "How would that make me look? I'm supposed to be a gentleman."

Despite the predicament she was in and despite the pain she was enduring, she thought bitterly, *You are probably too concerned about what others might think about you if they would find me lying here dead in the morning, half torn apart by wolves. After all, what would your precious high class friends think of you if word got around that you had refused to bring a lowly indentured servant girl to safety?*

The tall boy interrupted her thoughts. "The least I should do is take you along." With that said, he bent down and, picking her up in his arms, began to nearly jog towards the castle. Ignoring her vehement protests, he added, "As soon as we are return to the castle, I'll tell the cook to check your ankle."

Elizabeth seethed inwardly.

What a brute! How dare he carry her without asking permission!

The rotten rogue.

He was the boy she had always known he was. He had no respect to her as a person. He considered her dense and ignorant. He thought her illiterate.

The contrary rat!

If she could, she would wail on his hide so hard he wouldn't know what hit him.

All those years she had worked with his father on literature and mathematics. All those times she had spent sitting up for hours as the clock had struck past midnight. All the times she had worked on the books Noah Harrison had given her to study. She had passed them all with flying colors! And now…now this insolent boy picked her up as though she were a child! He treated her as though she were not important. She ought to tan his hide good. Tan his hide so good that there wouldn't be enough tar and feather! Or better yet, she would simply tell Noah Harrison exactly what she thought of his good-for-nothing laggard of a son. No doubt the poor man would die of a heart attack if she would ever tell him all the mean and hateful tricks the boy had played on her.

No, Elizabeth decided, horror flooding her at the thought. She would not tell the poor old man anything about what his son had done. She wouldn't say a single word. Instead, she'd do everything in her power to keep the old lord alive until her remaining years were up.

"Almost there now," David said suddenly, and Elizabeth heard relief in his voice. She was just as grateful. Her ankle throbbed dreadfully, and she was also terribly worried. She imagined the old man waiting with a heart of longing to see his son one last time before leaving earth.

She loved Noah Harrison. He was like a father to her. Why was her entire world shattering into thousands of pieces? Why was everyone she loved being taken away?

Her former tears again slipped down her cheeks but she ducked her head so that David wouldn't see them.

———

David rushed into the kitchen. His nurse and cook from when he was a child stood at the counter peeling potatoes for dinner. Her name was Rose, but when David had been a child he'd always called her 'Cook-Rose', and the name had just stuck.

"Cook-Rose, would you mind to please tend Beth's ankle? I think she's sprained it."

Rose gasped and whirled around. When she saw the two of them, however, she heaved a sigh. "Goodness, you startled me!"

David apologized quickly and Elizabeth noticed the surprise in the woman's eyes at his courtesy. The cook realized who the tall young man in front of her was, and her tone of voice changed to respect.

"What was that you asked, sir?"

David repeated his question, this time adding, "Beth says my father is desperately requesting my presence. I must go to him now."

The woman nodded. "Yes, sir, of course. Put her down on the

chair there and I will tend to her." She indicated with a hand towards a little rickety chair in the corner of the kitchen. David must have calculated roughly for he looked about himself in confusion before catching a glimpse of it and walking towards it.

"Thank you," he said as set her down on a chair. "I appreciate your help." He met the woman's eyes seriously as he said this, and Elizabeth was left with surprise at the sincere expression upon his face. She had never thought to see the day when he would take time to converse with a cook! Then again, she was the one who fed him.

The girl sniffed. That was undoubtedly the only reason. If David were to aggravate the cook, she could very well poison him!

The tall man offered a small smile at the woman's protestations that it was all her pleasure, and then rushed from the room.

The woman looked at Elizabeth, her expression relaying unabashed shock. "Why, I never thought to see the day that the mischievous young boy I used to take care of would grow up and become as fine a man as the one I just saw in front of me." Remembering why the girl was in her kitchen, the cook drew back her shoulders. "Sprained your ankle, did you? Which foot is it?"

Elizabeth jerked out of her mesmerism. "The left, ma'am," she replied.

The woman gently put her hand on the painful foot and carefully moved it. The girl flinched, and the cook immediately released it. "That's a pretty nasty sprain. Let me wrap it up."

Rose went over to a cupboard. When she returned, she was holding a white cloth. Elizabeth bit back swelling tears as her ankle was carefully wrapped with the cloth.

"Finished," the woman announced as she gently patted the cloth to make sure it wouldn't come loose. "But you won't be able to walk on this foot for a while."

"H…how how long?" Elizabeth breathed, feeling sick inside.

"About a month, depending on how badly it was sprained." Seeing the stricken look on her patient's face, she reassured her. "Now don't you fret, honey, you'll be fine."

But Elizabeth *had* to fret. Who wouldn't if they were in her predicament? She was indentured. And being indentured meant that if she were to become sick and couldn't work, those days would simply add onto the days on her contract.

Elizabeth didn't want to burden Rose with her thoughts so she simply nodded and tried for a smile instead. "I'll try not to."

The woman smiled at Annette's daughter. "Good. You can sit here if you want while I work on supper. I'd like to have a nice chat with you."

"Thank you, but no. I believe I'll try going to my room. I can't do anything until Mr. Harrison tells me what to do anyways, and since he's so ill…" Elizabeth faltered.

Cook-Rose nodded and rested her hand on the girl's shoulder in sympathy. "I know," she said sadly. "I've seen this coming a while already. I had a deep fear that he'd have a crash soon but didn't expect it to happen this fast." She sighed and picked up her knife to continue chopping carrots.

Elizabeth nodded, carefully rising while holding onto the counter-ledge. Gingerly, she hopped on her right foot to the door. When she was out of the kitchen, she limped into the marble hallway, and then breathing a deep sigh, wondered how she would get herself out of this predicament.

Chapter Four

North West Territories, Canada

Lemuel Ellis Keagan's burden was so heavy upon his mind and soul. Oh, how he wished he could release the rocks of guilt he carried. But his oppression remained just as back breaking and painful as ever. How he longed to give up his life's toll and find true peace and contentedness. But how could he? Was he lost to eternal damnation?

Oh yes, Lemuel knew about God. He knew about heaven and hell. In fact, he had been raised in a Christian family. However, as the years continued to slip by, his spirit had rebelled against God. He'd left his family at eighteen and went out to discover the world. He had wanted to live life to the fullest, not thinking about the consequences to his deeds. Yet now years later, the elderly man had a longing to tell someone about his past, but he was afraid of the consequences that were sure to follow his penitence.

If he did tell anyone his past and all his condoning deeds, he knew what would happen. *Most likely be a hangin'.* He could imagine the noose settling about his neck like iron and suddenly it being jerked tight. There wouldn't be any more air. He'd be dangling in the air by a cord of rope. Dead. Strangled to death.

He suddenly shivered and looked about himself, perhaps expecting to see a force of North West Mounted Police. Of course there was no one there. Feeling somewhat foolish, he straightened his shoulders and inhaled. He mentally scolded himself for being such an idiot. After all, no one knew his terrible secret. But would they ever find it out? Would the secret he carried one day be laid open for the world to see? He suppressed the urge to shiver and fervently hoped not.

———

London, England

David hurried towards his father's chamber, thoughts ricocheting through his head like hail on a tin roof. He pulled open his father's door and strode inside before stopping short as he saw a man near his father's side. When he recognized who it was, he quietly continued towards the bed. The doctor nodded respectfully before he turned and left the room, offering privacy.

"Father?" he whispered hoarsely. Seeing the old man's figure lying prone upon the bed, his heart lurched slightly. At his father's gesture, he proceeded to sit down on a chair nearby.

"David?" Noah coughed. "You are here. I was…I was not sure whether I could wait for you any longer. I am going to go directly to the point. There is not much time left."

David nodded, swallowing hard.

"I want you to do what you feel is right with this castle and everything in it. Everything but one thing is yours. Everything except your mother's sapphire ring. I want you to give it to Elizabeth." His father opened his hand and gently placed the ring into David's palm. Noah watched as his son fingered Victoria's wedding ring. The ring's brilliant blue stone glistened and sparkled as a ray of sunlight reached the tip of it. The gold band surrounding it shone vibrantly.

David remembered holding his mother's hand when he'd been a little boy and fingering her ring just as he was now.

Only this time there was no fingers to hold upon. Just the cold metal of her ring.

A dull ache squeezed his heart as David thought about her. Even in her darkest moments, she had never failed to offer an encouraging word to someone in need. Always providing comfort and sympathy to people around her, she had been the living example of how a Christian ought to live.

The tall man broke out of his reverie and nodded decisively, feeling another deep pin prick of remorse for the sick man in front of him. "Of course, I will give it to her."

Noah drew a deep breath. He cleared his throat; his breathing became ragged. "Thank you. Now for Elizabeth…"

David swallowed hard. What was his father getting at? He nodded with a quick inclination of his head for his father to continue.

"After her mother's death, I taught that girl how to read and write, taught her mathematics and etiquette." The old man's voice broke. "I think of Elizabeth as my own daughter. Now that I am going, I am frightened for her. She is only fourteen yet. Who will look out for her when I am gone?" He again coughed, and then continued, exhaling a ragged breath.

"Her contract ends when she is nineteen. She has a spirit that must not be broken, David. She is a unique girl. I ask of you to please take care of her. Protect her. She is all alone in this world and in her young innocence she will not realize the dangers of unsavory people that will wish to take advantage of her."

What? His father wanted him to take care of Elizabeth? What was he thinking?! *Isn't he aware that Beth and I aren't on good terms?*

David looked at his father's white face. The dull black eyes silently pleaded with hope. And at the moment he knew he couldn't deny his father's silent plea. He nodded decisively. "Yes, Father."

His father drew another feeble breath. "I was wrong in making her work. I was just so swept along with the culture around me, so swayed by others' say-so, oh, I was such an ignoramus fool. But now that I am dying, there really isn't any use in attempting to condone and overlook my behavior. Times are changing, David. Do what you know to be right. Do not look towards any man but look only to God. Stand by the truth, stand by righteousness. Stand by integrity."

David shook his head in earnest. "Father, I have always stood by integrity. You ought to not worry about Beth. I will look after her like I would to my own sister!"

The old man closed his eyes in sadness. "Yes, I know you will. But that does not change the way I have treated her. She should have been made a lady of this castle. Even after her mother passed away, she shouldn't have worked another day in her life. She is a good girl…" A rare smile tugged at his pale lips. "Just very outspoken and impulsive." The smile vanished, regret replacing it. "Tell her… without hesitation, David; tell her I'm a fool. Oh yes, the world's greatest fool."

"Father, you did what you thought best." David felt a lump fill his throat. Why was this conversation so heartbreaking? Because both men knew that Noah Harrison was saying his last farewell?

Oh, dear Lord. Don't take my father away yet. Please give me some time to be with him before his time has come when he leaves us all.

But his father continued, shaking his head. "What I thought best? Oh yes, I *thought* I was doing the best thing I possibly could under the circumstances. I had a choice but I made the wrong one. In my heart I wanted to free her from the indenture papers. But what would everyone else think if I were to do that? I would not only have other lords upset with me but also my own jealous servants!" Noah shook his head once more. "Regardless, I did not do best. I should have done what I *knew* was the right thing to do. Instead, I allowed my fellow humans around me to pull me with strings in the direction of their selfish beliefs. I was wrong. Dear God, I was so wrong!" The old man closed his eyes, a tear slipping from the corner. "And now it is too late for a change. I am dying and it is too late to amend this mistake. Oh, I have been such a fool!"

The old man's words struck a cord within David's soul. He reached out a hand towards the dying man. "Father, we all make mistakes. When we realize those mistakes, however, we are coming to grips with our sinful nature."

Noah Harrison sighed. "Ah yes, we all make mistakes. But how I wish that we would not make them. Would not life be so much easier to live if there was no such thing as a mistake?"

The lord's voice was despondent. David did not quite know how to respond to his father's words.

Noah Harrison looked as though the oppression of all the world's sorrows was upon his shoulders, weighing him down. He shook his head forlornly.

"Your mother's ring is for her. I want her to have something special to express my appreciation for her devotion to this old man." Noah rasped for a breath.

David swallowed. "What are you saying, Father? What about Beth?"

But his father only shook his head. "It is the end now for me. But Elizabeth!" He looked into his son's eyes. "She is not who you think she is. She is…is not the title you think she is. She…" The old man choked, coughing again.

David rested a hand upon his father's shoulder. "Are you all right?" Fear evinced in his tone.

Noah shook his head. "David, forget me. I am leaving you. Elizabeth is important here."

David grimaced. "No, Father, *you* are the one important."

The lord frowned. "Son, listen to my words. Promise me you won't forget them. They are the key for the future. For *her* future. Elizabeth is not all who you may deem her to be."

David nodded impatiently. "All right, what about her?"

"Promise me that you will remember my words! Her father…" Noah gasped for his last breath before his chest suddenly became still.

"Doctor!" David cried helplessly.

The physician rushed into the room. He grasped Noah's hand, feeling for a pulse. But it was too late. The tall man sat in silence, unabashed by the tears coursing down his cheeks in the dark room.

Chapter Five

Footsteps in the hall caused Elizabeth to look up. David Harrison walked up slowly, exhaustion she had never before seen there etched upon his face. He stopped in front of her, his eyes betraying a look of something unexplainable. Something that made her heart lurch. Was his father worse?

"Can you come to the garden? I need to tell you something and it is of the utmost importance." He lifted a shaky hand towards his forehead, and then blew out his breath. "Oh, I forgot about your ankle. How is it?"

Elizabeth could see directly through the question. He didn't really care about her foot and had only asked because had to know if she could make it to the garden. Fear eased its way into her heart as she remembered her sore limb. She really didn't want any extra days added to her contract. Could she work even though her ankle was sprained? She sincerely doubted that.

"It is only a minor sprain."

He looked at her quizzically. "How long will you be off your feet?"

The girl swallowed hard. "Uh…Cook-Rose says that I'll be laid up for about a month."

He nodded. "I see. May I carry you to the garden if you are unable to walk such a long distance? It is urgent that I speak to you at once alone."

She opened her mouth to spurn his request but quickly closed it again. Curiosity prompted her to dip her head and reluctantly concur.

He carried her outside to the gardens walking slowly, deep in thought. She wished he would hurry up as she was just aching to hear his urgent message. When they finally reached the gardens, David gently lowered her onto a bench. He sat across from her on a tree stump, elbows upon his knees, head lowered, and hands in his hair.

He was acting very peculiar, she thought, eyeing him in surprise. Never before had she seen the arrogant David Harrison act so weary and melancholy. She was prepared for whatever news he had.

"My father just passed away to his eternal rest."

A small cry escaped Elizabeth before she could quench it. She bit her lip to keep back the tears that welled within her deep green eyes. No! Not dear Mr. Harrison.

The tears fell hard.

The tall man cleared his throat, awkwardness settling over his features as he spoke the words that warmed her very heart and soul. She drank in each word he spoke, her pale and tear-streaked features stupefied with amazement.

"Father asked me to tell you that he loves you and that he thought of you as his own daughter. He told me to give you my mother's ring…" He dug into his pocket and pressed the beautiful band into the palm of her outstretched hand.

Elizabeth's eyes widened with surprise before a look of pure wonder followed. She held the glittering blue ring in her hand and turned it around and around in awe. The deceased lord was giving such a valuable item to her? Lowly, poor, homely Elizabeth Davison?

For one thrilling moment, she envisioned herself wearing the treasured piece of jewelry before all the *ton* of England, and excitement flooded her as she imagined seeing their shocked expressions as she daintily flaunted her glittering finger about. Imagined being swept off her feet by a handsome knight and twirled around the ballroom in a green gown of lace and satin. She smiled for one moment, despite the sadness that tore at another part of her heart. If Noah Harrison were still alive, she was sure he would smile at her with encouragement. His gentle smile always seemed to make her soar like an eagle.

But then she shook herself. No, she couldn't accept the ring. She *wouldn't* accept it. It was too…beautiful. Too beautiful for her.

When she looked up, tears pooled her eyes once more.

"I-I am not good enough to take it. I'm not good enough to possess such a beautiful ring. It was your mother's, after all." She glanced up into his eyes, searching for an answer.

The tall man was surprised by her response. "My father requested you have it. As you were like a daughter to my father, this is directed specifically to you as a token of appreciation."

She averted her gaze, moistening her parched lips. "Yes, but I don't know what to do with it right at the moment. I am afraid I might lose or break it. You know my tendency for clumsiness. I really think you ought to keep it for me, at least for the present."

David nodded slowly. He was reluctant in agreeing but her pleading made up his mind. "All right, Beth. I will keep it for you for now. Whenever you wish for it to be returned, let me know."

Elizabeth braved a smile. "Thank you."

"My father asked me to take care of you because he said you were too young to be on your own. He asked me to be your guardian until you are nineteen years old. I agreed."

Everything David continued to say blurred out into the backgrounds. She didn't hear another word from his lips.

She. Was. Fuming.

She now 'belonged' to David Harrison, her enemy. He would boast and brag and probably tell her to work faster and harder. He would doubtlessly *add* another entire month to her contract for not being able to work because of her ankle. Maybe even an entire year!

But David continued. "I don't agree with owning people. Although I never voiced my disapproval when my father participated with the practice, I always vowed that when I would inherit this castle as my own I'd never own indentured servants. I believe one should not be owned by another man. I am calling off all the contracts with the indentured servants, but…" He hedged for time before speaking the inevitable. "Father asked me to be your guardian until you are nineteen to which I agreed."

Elizabeth's throat congested. A guardian. He was now her guardian. Ha! Not that she required anyone watching over her. She was just as strong and smart as him. She could easily protect herself.

The controlling bigot.

Then disappointment swooped over her. Even though he was her guardian, she knew that she would still be required to work for five years. Five terribly long, boring years in *his* castle with an egoistic creature that was intent upon making her life miserable.

Tears gathered within her burning eyes. Her rage returned. All the horrible things he had done through all the years resurfaced. How could he be anything but the bigot he was? She had never been so angry before. Well, perhaps when he had slipped a frog into her shoe and made her nearly murder it. The memory in itself brought a rush of sizzling fury as the realization flooded her that, like always, she was helpless to defend herself or to call him out his behavior.

It appeared David had noticed her resentment for he spoke gently.

"Beth, don't be upset. My father is right; you really are too young to be on your own. But it will be different. You won't be indentured; you will be like a younger sister to me."

Elizabeth had no words. She gazed at David in utter bewilderment. She had never known him to be so grown up! Here was a side of him she'd never before seen.

Her lack of response was just fine with him. Sometimes it was better having her quiet. And other times…well, it was not.

———

David Harrison leaned back in his chair, threading his hands behind his head. Now that he had resolved to authorize freedom to every indentured person, he decided that he needed to develop a formulated design for his subsequent future.

I could sell the castle and move to Canada, and be something other than a lord as I have always secretly wanted. Disappointment flooded him. *That won't work because of Beth. I can't abandon because I am in charge of her. I promised Father I would take care of her and I will keep that promise to him, no matter what.*

He cleared his throat. An idea took charge and he veered ahead before he even realized what he was thinking. He would ask Cook-Rose to care for her. Surely the woman wouldn't mind. She had been, after all, a good friend of Elizabeth's mother.

Now his plan seemed complete.

Except the fact, however, that he still had to find a way to tell Elizabeth.

———

"What?" Elizabeth stared at the tall young man, not fully comprehending what he had just stated. "What did you just say?"

"I just said that I'm going to ask Cook-Rose to care for you." He sighed. "Listen, Beth, I want to move away from here. I want a new life! I want freedom. I don't want to be a lord. I don't want indentured servants. What I want is…"

Elizabeth rolled her eyes, interrupting him. "I know, I know. You want a new life. The only unfortunate problem is that I am causing you a dilemma. You promised your father that you'd care for me, but now you want to leave England and go to a different country. And it would all work out perfectly, except for one little obstacle positioned directly in your path. Me."

Elizabeth crossed her arms against her chest, waiting to hear his response. Now that she was free, she didn't concern herself with how she spoke to him. It didn't matter anymore. There could be no punishments or sharp scoldings now. And after only a few days, she had soon discovered David didn't really care how she spoke to him either. All those words that had bubbled within her heart of past years erupted like a volcano. It felt so satisfying to have the opportunity to argue. Oh, how she loved every moment of her beautiful freedom!

David shook his head and frowned in exasperation. "No, that is not it. *You* are not the problem. It is just that Canada is no place for a girl to live. It will be dangerous and"

"You inveigle boy! The place you are going is not dangerous at all; you only say it as an excuse to frighten me. And the part of me being a girl…it's absurd!"

Elizabeth was enraged. He was trying to make excuses to get rid of her; she was certain of it now. What a blind fool she had been to even think that David Harrison would ever even consider fulfilling his promise to his dead father!

David glared at her. He appeared frustrated. "Beth, open your eyes. You are putting blinders on to make yourself believe something that is not true! It is dangerous; why would I deceive you? And quite frankly, it is really quite simple to draw the conclusion that you are weaker than a man. This is just an obvious fact that you have to face. I have heard you say that you can do anything a man can. However, you must realize that God made a difference."

Elizabeth could not believe what she was hearing. Anger unfurled and she gritted her teeth. "*'Weaker than a man?'*" She all but squeaked the words. "How dare you say such a thing, you bubbleheaded, rude boy! I do not try to show you that I am stronger than a man or anything. You are putting words into my mouth. Oh, and you think God made a difference in between both a man and a woman?" She scoffed openly. "Don't be ridiculous. There is no God!"

"I beg your pardon?" he questioned dubiously. "Did I just hear you announce that there is no God?"

"Yes, you did," she spit back. "My mother always told me that He hears us when we pray or when we seek guidance, but where is

He now? I have cried to Him for years but there is never an answer." Tears filled her eyes, unbidden, but she sniffed them back. "I kept waiting for His answer but none ever came. And I have now come upon the conclusion that there isn't a God. At least, I hope there isn't any. Why would He ignore me? He left me alone to my own devices. And now now I will leave Him alone as well. We shall both disregard each other. If that is the way He wants it, fine, I will also ignore Him."

The tall man's heart sank at her words. She was bitter inside. Bitter and angry. David could hear it in her tone. He shook his head, eyes filled with disbelief. Was this the Elizabeth he always used to tease? When had she gotten so bitter?

"How can you turn your back upon Him? How can you even voice the thoughts you entertain about there not being a God? He did not ignore you when you cried to Him for help. He heard every word you spoke, yet sometimes God will not answer your request in the way you think or want Him to."

David Harrison's voice was filled with such urgency. He almost sounded as though he meant what he was saying to her! A small trickle of hope spread throughout her veins. Could he really mean it?

Ridiculous thought.

She banished it from her mind. That ill-mannered lout was probably trying to make her believe he really meant it when he didn't.

His explicit voice broke into her thoughts. "... And He has either answered you already and you have just not heard His voice, or He will answer your supplication in a way you never intended. But I promise that He heard you."

Elizabeth gaped at him in obvious shock. "I-I concede. I-I do think there is a God. However, I am certain He does not regard my miserable existence one way or another. He hates and despises me with a vengeance and has already bid me *au revoir* without a second glance."

"He has not deserted you and He is still beside you, helping you every step of the way. Can you not believe that His presence is everywhere?"

She shrugged, her fire returning. "That sounds particularly absurd." With a toss of her head, she met his eyes defiantly. "I've already made my decision. Stop preaching to me!"

His jaw tightened. "I'm not preaching, Beth. I'm trying to help you."

She scoffed at that. "Help me? It's more like hinder me, isn't it? You hate me. I wouldn't be surprised to hear that you also wish I were dead along with my mother."

David's eyes widened with shock. "Don't say such things!" he snapped. "Why would I wish you dead?"

She moistened her parched lips. Anger tinged his tone. Was it a warning? She gulped. But she had come just too far to back out. Especially now. He would think he had frightened her as usual. Not that he hadn't, but she refused to admit it.

She kicked up her chin a notch. "Is that so?" she replied vindictively. "Despite what you say, I am not a beggar."

"What a strange thing to say, Beth," David returned disapprovingly. "I've never once insinuated you were a beggar. The only thing you beg is love and acceptance."

She gasped. "What do you mean?"

"Just that. You crave love. You crave acceptance, validation, and respect. You allow your own insecurities to drown your potential, and you argue with me because it makes you feel better about yourself." His mouth tipped up most exasperatingly. "But if it makes you feel any better, I really don't mind to be your scapegoat."

Her chest heaved with rage. "D-David Harrison!" she shrieked. "You horrible, rude, nasty boy! How dare you say such egoistic, arrogant words to me?"

He chuckled. "Did it ever occur to you that I don't hate you?"

Elizabeth frowned. "Wh-what?" Confusion etched her brow. Not hate her? That ill-mannered lout? She flipped her head. No, certainly not. That man wouldn't even care if she were falling off a cliff. In fact, he'd probably deliberately pry her fingers off the cliff's ledge and watch her fall down into the dark depths of the raging ocean below.

She shivered as her dark imagination appeared to follow the path of a tunnel, deeper and deeper into loathing antipathy. Straightening, she glowered at him and pressed her lips together in outrage. "I hate you!" she exclaimed, unable to come up with another suitable response. "Did you hear me? I hate you!"

His eyes darkened at her statement but he didn't answer. The moment the words spilled from her mouth, regret flooded her. But it was too late. The words had been spoken. She couldn't retrieve them. And since she was too proud to apologize, she lifted her head with a forced dignity and met his gaze squarely.

Chapter Six

"If you think I will merely sit back and watch you step aboard the ship without a word of protest, your logic is flawed!" she hissed. "Despite what you may think, I am certainly not a ninny. *However,*" she paused, setting a finger against her lips and gazing off into the distance thoughtfully, "if you tell me why you intend to leave me behind here, I may concede."

They stood facing each other in the corridor. A long, awkward silence ensued. Instead of glancing away from his piercing gaze, Elizabeth met his gaze defiantly, her green eyes blazing with determination. David gritted his teeth with frustration, and then sighed. "All right, then. I suppose it wouldn't be so terrible if you were to come along," he mused.

"But..." Elizabeth stared at him, both astonishment and horror bouncing through her mind. This was not at all what she had intended. She had merely wanted him to affirm her suspicions that he had planned to get out of his promise to his father by dumping her. She didn't actually want to go along...right?

She pressed her lips together tightly. No, she didn't. She determined to stay in England where she belonged. She would not go across the ocean to a land she had never known or seen. How ridiculous! Had that David Harrison finally gone round the twist?

The tall man shook his head. "Actually..." A smile plagued his lips as a plan formed. Since Elizabeth abhorred being instructed about, he would do just that. The poor thing would recoil instantly.

He set his jaw and steeled his tone. "On second thought, I will need a domestic to assist me along the journey. As you often point out, I really am not accustomed to a life without a personal drudge." He slanted her a smug grin. "I order you to accompany me."

Her head reared back with horror. "No, I will certainly not be your menial slave. I refuse to."

He feigned a frown. "It does not matter if you do not wish to go. You are going because I said you are going."

The girl gaped. "But...but I thought you were just telling me that you did not desire my company!"

"I changed my mind. You made me see the logic in your words. I quite require a servant." He smiled plainly as if she were a nonsensical child. "I am leaving in about half a year. I must sell this castle and arrange for immigration papers so you have a while to acclimate to the idea."

She huffed for air, face scrunched. "I refuse to come. You shall have to drag me aboard the ship first."

He threw back his head and laughed at that. "Then I shall drag you. You brought this upon yourself, Beth. You wanted to come along? All right, you will come along."

She gulped. She knew his tone enough over the years to understand that he had made up his mind. But she also was not one to give up. Grasping for her last option, she licked her dry lips. "Very well, if you insist, sir." She hung her head, her gaze lowering to the floor to mimic that of a loyal, respectful servant. It made her blood boil to have to resort to such a submissive posture to such an egoistic, arrogant man. "It is just that I thought I heard you declare that I am now free." She subdued the anger in her tone to a honeyed plea.

He lifted her chin with his fingers so she was forced to look up. "Don't question my decisions, scullion," he made himself growl. He grinned as she jerked her chin out of his grip and glared at him just as he had expected, her green eyes flashing.

"Do you perhaps have the tendency to change your mind abruptly?" she demanded, her eyes dripping resentment. "I am sure you are already aware of this, but a gentleman never relinquishes his word."

"There are many different types of 'gentlemen' in this world," he replied calmly. "As I am sure you are also aware, I do not fall beneath any particular category. As a result I have the ability to effectively control various situations. How you act is where I determine how to respond." He flashed an impudent grin before he then asked if he should accompany her to her room.

She frowned. Why, that uncouth boy. What a nerve! She was about to scream with outrage, but at that moment a maid walked by. Elizabeth's voice was coated with artificial sugar. "Yes, thank you. That would indeed be much appreciated, most gallant sir."

Ignoring her sarcastic tone of voice, the tall man grinned slightly. "Don't worry about it, my dear lady."

The maid had past. The act was off instantly. Just as Elizabeth was about to hurl back a most rude comeback, the laundry maid marched by with laundry piled higher than her head. She careened around the corner of the hallway nearly crashing directly into both David and Elizabeth.

David played the well-acted part of a gentleman. He straightened to his full height and pasted on a smile. Steadying the flustered maiden by her elbow, the tall man bowed gallantly. "Are you all right, miss?"

The poor girl looked shocked into near paralyzation. She swallowed hard. "Uh…yes, sir. I am fine, sir. Thank you, sir."

David Harrison raised an eyebrow. "I apologize for standing in the way."

The girl swallowed again. Her eyes were that of a doe wary of danger, and she looked ready to bolt at any sudden movement. She eyed them surreptitiously, more so Elizabeth, her eyes casting up and down at the girl's look and manner of dress and then after muttering another stream of apologies, meekly clutched the white linen, and then continued on her way with the now not-so-neat pile of laundry.

Elizabeth Davison sniffed disdainfully as David Harrison

crooked his arm out for her to lay hand upon it. Reluctantly, she laid her hand upon his arm and then limped down the hall, attempting desperately to keep up with the tall young man at her side.

Humiliated as she passed numerous servants doing their duties, her face burned as red as a ripe tomato as they all turned to stare at both her and David. No doubt they were astounded to see an indentured servant walking with the son of their deceased lord. She offered a tentative smile and attempted to remove the distasteful frown upon her lips. Oh, but wouldn't this bring tongues to wag!

Of course she knew David had only asked because she had a sprained ankle and it was difficult to walk without a steadying hand. Yet to walk among all the servants she worked with daily, her hand upon his arm…why, the very idea was humiliating! She was sure that David Harrison knew that as well. But why would he attempt to shame and disgrace her? Why would he want all her fellow servants to whisper among themselves that there was perhaps something going on between the well regarded lord's son and a lowly indentured servant girl?

The answer hit her full in the face.

It was all because he *wanted* to embarrass her. Why was she even surprised? David Harrison had always been a thorn in her side. That had never changed. He was a hateful brute; a miserable excuse for being the offspring of the kind late Noah Harrison.

Elizabeth stumbled. She shot him an irritated, incensed look. He was deliberately mortifying her! She was certain of it. He was deliberately walking his fast stride, probably secretly hoping she would fall flat on her face. Well, she wouldn't. She would hold her head high and walk in his stride because she refused to be the subject of his mocking gaze. Not one more minute would she permit his condescending behavior to continue.

The rogue. Just rotten to his very core. She guessed icy water ran through his veins. He had a heart made of stone and definitely did not contain a conscience within his miserable being.

He turned down another hall, and then began to walk down a

few flats. She struggled after him, nearly pitching down the stairs at every step.

Was it her fault her poor short limbs were unable to keep in stride with his long legs? No, she decided swiftly. David Harrison was completely held liable for behaving so rudely. Courtesy pointed to at least *respecting* someone. Decorous manners directed one's complete attention and gracious character present at all times. Why did he treat her like a slave?

She was suddenly jerked forwards. Apparently, she had been walking too slowly. Did the man not have the ability to remember that she had injured her ankle?

Anger unfurled within her veins. She curled her fingers into her palms. And how dare that uncouth, boorish David Harrison abruptly declare he was going to Canada and that she was going with? The very idea was as preposterous as it sounded.

Absurd.

She, Elizabeth Hannah Davison, boarding a ship and going across the ocean and to an unknown land? She wouldn't be seen doing it even if it were the last place to go to on earth! A thought occurred to her. It could even be true that there was no such thing as Canada! Perhaps people had merely invented it as a joke to fool innocent people! What if David was being deceived by thinking the 'land of milk and honey' was real when in reality it wasn't? What if he would arrive to nothing?

She threw back her shoulders, or at least tried to as they hurried along.

Ha! Well, he deserved it. That antagonizing son of Noah Harrison *deserved* to end up in the middle of nowhere! He deserved to be deceived.

As she recalled his son's demanding words that she was going along with him to Canada regardless of her consent, she countered back, bitterness washing over her. He would have to drag her first. Drag her by her hair for all she cared.

She blinked at that thought.

But what if he were so determined that he *did* pull her by her hair down the streets to the ship? She frowned. What about her hair? What if he accidentally or deliberately pulled all her hair out as well as the roots? Wouldn't she be bald for the rest of her life, then?

She pursed her lips. If she really had to go along to Canada, she would prefer to have her hair still intact than to look ridiculous and be bald. Besides, what was holding her back from going to the land called Canada? Her pride?

There was nothing here for her in England anyways. Hadn't she overheard some townspeople talking about Canada and how the country had a profusion of gold? Memories resurfaced as she recalled one man standing and holding a newspaper in his hand. She remembered espying a drawing of an elegant and prestigious lady in the left corner. The woman had been wearing a beautiful lace dress; one Elizabeth had always imagined wearing regally. Couldn't she wear one of these if she would go to Canada?

Excitement furrowed through her. Of course she could if she were to merely take the journey across the ocean and to Canada. She could become rich and maybe she could even have a few servants of her own! Her mind cleared of any doubts it had entertained. Completely forgetting David's command that she was coming along, she swiftly made her decision. She would show that David Harrison that she could do whatever he did!

When they arrived at the door of her room, she jerked her hand off of his arm and then glared up at him. The tall man smiled inveterately at her. "Aren't you going to thank me for taking you down all these steps?"

"Of course not!" she snapped. "Besides, you already told me that I wasn't to think anything more of the topic of you escorting me." Narrowing her eyes, she twisted her lip like the cat that got the cream. "And just for the record, I didn't need any help either. I only *permitted* you to be of 'assistance' for your sake so you wouldn't get hurt or offended."

He snorted. "I don't get offended easily and certainly not hurt."

Irritation flooded her. That was probably what most frustrated her. His smooth confidence.

"Liar!" she nearly shouted.

His mouth opened slightly in shock at the vehemence in her tone. "What did you call me?" he asked, his tone of voice ominous.

She gulped. "W-well, what I really meant to say was that I have *decided* to accompany you to Canada. I'll even be your personal drudge."

The tall man gawked. "You want to go?" He could not believe what he was hearing.

She nodded. "I…" There was a slight hesitation before she lifted her chin and spoke unflinchingly. "Yes, I do. But could you…I mean, if you don't mind to pay for my passage west." She looked up at him expectantly, partially concerned that he would pull her hair out of her head right now.

David sighed inwardly. Everything was back-firing. Although she now appeared eager, what could he say? He had been expecting her to continue pouting and then last minute tell her he had changed his mind. Now it was too late. He decided to make the best of it.

"What a silly question, Beth." He forced a smirk. "I thought I already informed you that you are accompanying me so of course I will pay your passage."

She smiled at him smugly, not even appearing enraged at his irritatingly smug expression. "I shall wait the day when we can sail to Canada in anticipation."

The tall man groaned inwardly but smiled outwardly before turning away. As he retraced his steps back up the flat of stairs, he was filled with the knowledge that his plan had backfired right into his own face.

———

Elizabeth clasped her hands together.

to Canada to the dangerous land. She would survive. She could do it.

She would show that arrogant, opinionated, swaggering, boastful, blustering, patronizing, lordly, imperious, mocking, sneering, scoffing, pompous Mr. David Harrison a thing or two before the year was done, all right!

Sighing in satisfaction, she settled onto her bed. Propping up her aching ankle, she soon lost herself in her own turmoil of thoughts.

That David Harrison really thought he was something. *Self-centered bigot,* she huffed. *Oh, how I hate his superior air of confidence!*

Couldn't he see how she was feeling? He had thrown something at her without even pausing to consider her opinion on the subject! She was already distraught with the knowledge that her lord was deceased when suddenly David was giving her the thrilling news that she was free from her indentured papers. It was all so sudden. *Too* sudden. There were so many mixed emotions. She wanted to cry. She wanted to laugh. But most of all, she wanted to sob against her mother's shoulder. To just be held. All she wanted was someone to offer her comfort. But now there was no one. Why did it seem as though all her loved ones or friends were wrestled away from her? Besides that David Harrison, of course. She wrinkled her nose. But she wouldn't touch him with a thirty-nine-and-a-half-foot-pole! He was an insufferable man with a most condescending, lofty attitude that had her nearly casting her accounts.

She bit her lip. Well, she would show him a thing or two yet!

That David Harrison would see that she was a warrior. A fierce warrior. She would break forth into the battlefield with her sword and her shield and valiantly fight for her dignity. She would be courageous and proud. She would never back down from anything, including him. Actually, *especially* him.

She was a warrior, after all. She could withstand anything.

Watch me, she thought defiantly. *Just watch me.*

ant44

Chapter Seven

Nearly a year later

Elizabeth inhaled deeply. She had been on the *Lady Diana* for two weeks already, and she loved the air! It was so beautiful out at sea with those fresh, intoxicating salty waves crashing up against the ship. She gazed across the spread of the Atlantic Ocean, thinking about the land she was going to. A land she knew nothing about; a land that was unknown. Was she doing the right thing?

The date was March 13, 1894. She had turned sixteen in September when they still had both been in England. It was indeed grown-up, she decided, thinking yet again of what a great and important age that was. *Sixteen!* she thought. *I am no longer a child but a young lady. Oh, doesn't that age just inspire my soul?*

Her mind changed course suddenly as it always tended to do and she recalled when they had gotten aboard the *Lady Diana*.

———

On the 18th of May last year, they had gathered their meager amounts of luggage (David had been determined to take as little as possible and buy the necessary supplies once they would arrive) onto the large vessel by the ship's docking berth.

It had been a dreary day. The rain had poured down in sheets and the sky had been filled with a gloomy demeanor a lot like her thoughts. She had felt melancholy at leaving her native land. The land she had called home all her years, never once had she imagined she would have to leave. The thought hadn't even occurred to her.

Because she had been so obsessed with the fact that she was indentured last year, no other thought had even knocked upon her heart with the vision that her life could ever change. But when she began the voyage, it was different. She had known that it wasn't just a dream but that it was real. That she really was going to Canada and that she was finally free from the choking chains of indenture.

When the ship had begun to move, the literal lurch resonated within her, tearing at her heart. Elizabeth had begun to capture glimpses of what was going on around her. No longer was her vision shrouded by obscure scenes or shapes. It seemed that everything was so bright and vibrant compared to a few months earlier.

She and David turned as one to watch the land fade out of sight. A sudden sense of terror seized her soul. She fought the urge to scream, "Wait, I've changed my mind. Turn back around; I want to stay in England!" But of course she did not. She forced away the tears that had welled up into her eyes, blinking them back. She pulled strange faces to better accommodate the sobs that arose within her heart and soul. She was leaving England. She was going away. Undoubtedly to never return.

———

As she gazed out over the widespread of the Atlantic Ocean, apprehensiveness suddenly overwhelmed her being. She felt extremely small and vulnerable on a tiny dot of the ship in the midst of a gigantic ocean all around her. There was no land within view, nothing solid around her.

Elizabeth shivered. Perhaps she was being impulsive. Perhaps she ought to have stayed in England after all. But then another sensation bubbled from within her soul. Pride and determination. Courage. There was suddenly such staunch resolution in her soul that she was incognizant where it had stemmed from.

She would show that David Harrison she could do anything he professed she could not achieve. She was Elizabeth Hannah Davison. She was on her way to Canada. And she was going to become every bit of the Canadian David himself seemed to think she could never become!

"You still out here? Don't you think you ought to turn in?"

Elizabeth's eyes flew open and she jumped. Her heart beat wildly, tripping over itself with shock. In the shadows a tall figure stood. His imposing height and stance nearly frightened ten years out of her life. Elizabeth forced her fast-beating heart to slow as she realized that it was only David, the victim of her thoughts.

Upon seeing her frightened expression, his blue eyes twinkled. He took a deep breath, inhaling the salty breeze just as she had a few minutes before.

"It is quite a spectacular view out here on the ship, do you not agree?"

She did not reply.

He tried once again. "Still daydreaming, Beth?" He shook his head. "You really ought to accept life the way it is."

Now she glared at him. "There isn't necessarily a particular reason you must startle me in such a frightening manner. I could have fallen into the ocean and died!"

He shrugged nonchalantly. "Well, how else can I obtain your attention to listen to what I am trying to say? You generally ignore my words and so I have decided the best way to acquire a response is to startle you. Clever idea, is it not?"

Elizabeth gritted her teeth, irritated by his presence. She'd just been enjoying the quiet beauty of the water and the quiet serenity from solitude of the ocean when he had interrupted her thoughts. "I'd appreciate it if you'd mind your own business and leave me to mine," she snapped.

He frowned. "Unfortunately, I don't believe I can do such a thing. You see, I made a promise to my father that I would look out for you."

She kicked up her chin a notch. "Only until I turn nineteen," she returned haughtily.

His mouth twitched and she was sure he was fighting a smile. "The point is that I'm required to look after you until then. Let's focus on the present and not on the future."

"You must really enjoy dominating my life," she fumed, narrowing her eyes with malice.

He laughed then. "Believe what you desire, my lady. I won't deter you."

She shot him a mildly dirty scowl but allowed herself to crook her arm on his offered one. They then commenced to walking down the deck together in silence.

———

North West Territories, Canada

A twig snapped and he jumped. When he realized how he was acting, however, Lemuel Ellis Keagan forced himself to remain calm. After all, why did he have to be so jumpy about his surroundings?

He knew the answer. It was the answer that haunted him daily. It was because he didn't trust anything. He was certain that everything intended to make his life miserable. People always had devious designs in everything they did and said. Of that he was sure.

He steeled his jaw.

But he wouldn't let them. He'd had enough of their underhanded behaviors in his lifetime to last one hundred lives! He determined to never lower his defenses again. Not in anything or for anyone. Not ever. He'd learned his lesson. Granted, it had been a hard lesson to learn, but he had learned it. And it had cured him. Cured him forever.

Now he wanted to just continue living off the land and doing what he pleased. His life was no longer going to be ruled by anyone else. He'd live alone forever. It didn't matter if he was lonely. In his opinion, it was better to be alone than be used by others for their own selfish benefits. Besides, who really cared for him? Lemuel Ellis Keagan was unable to think of anyone who really cared for him except his grandson, Keith Winchester.

His last thought brought remorse to flood his soul. He really had been away from the boy far too long. The boy could be even dead at this time!

Get a grip on yourself, Keagan! Get back home and stay with him for the rest of your miserable life!

Another voice plagued his mind.

But you can't, can you? You know the reason why you are always hunting and trapping is because you are trying to run away. You are trying to run away from your conscience. You are trying to run away from responsibility.

Lemuel Ellis Keagan battled within himself. *No, that's not true! I ain't just tryin' to run away from Keith or responsibility. It's true that I am runnin' from my conscience of past wrongs, but I don't want to be with Keith so much. It hurts my soul. Whenever I look at the boy, I see Olivia…and how I miss her!*

A pang of sadness surged through him.

Olivia. Sweet, precious Olivia.

Why had the Lord taken Olivia, the only one who had ever truly understood him? God had whisked the star of his life away. She had been the child who had changed his life twenty five years ago. She had been the main factor in transforming him from being a cold-hearted outlaw who only cared for himself into a man worthy of self-respect. Just as Lemuel had seen a glimpse of peacefulness, she had been whisked away from him by God.

How Lemuel yearned to hear his daughter's twinkling laughter and to see her beautiful smile! Wistfulness for the sincere depths of her brown eyes haunted him. He wanted every little thing about her back. Oh, his sweet, darling Olivia. *Why?* he screamed. *Why did You take her from me? Wasn't takin' her husband good enough for You? What do You really want from me, God?!*

Childhood memories flashed through his mind of his mother praying with him before bedtime and his father telling him about how there were two choices a person could make and how that choice would affect your life forever.

A stab of regret slashed his heart. His father had pointed him in the right direction, but he had chosen the very opposite. He had taken it because he had been a lad filled with an arrogant, superior air that he was cleverer than his own father. He had taken to 'know the world' and had ended up with the wrong friends.

The young man had stolen, murdered, and lied. He had shot along with the best of his fellow outlaws. He'd been one of the best gunslingers in his gang. He had been a proud and contemptuous young man with a derisive attitude.

Back in those days, however, Lemuel had never thought of himself as that. He had been proud of being the cocky young outlaw, driven by the Evil One to prey upon others. He had swaggered around the towns and had lounged all about the gambling halls and saloons. He had lost all sense of religion and had become a regular unproductive outlaw.

But the boy hadn't cared. He had done what he had found good in his own eyes. Eventually, his cocksure manner had gotten the best of him. The band of notorious outlaws he had joined discarded him because he'd been too brazen and self-conceited.

Now penniless and alone, some of the puffed up bravado began to diminish. Wanted posters with his name printed in bold had him running. Passing town through town, he began to think about his family. How was his mother? Was she still praying for him? Was his stern father still working the fields? How was his little sister, Rose? The little girl who'd sobbed at his defiant announcement that he was leaving home for good? And how was his younger brother, Jeremiah? The boy who had revered everything Lemuel did?

Regret finally led him drifting back to the small town of Faro where he'd grown up. When he arrived at his family's homestead, horror bubbled up within him as he silently saw the shambles before him. What had happened in his absence?

A neighbor confirmed his fears. They had all taken sick with a deadly influenza that had swept through the town.

At that moment, something had broken within him. He had sank down to the ground, sobbing. Even as a grown man, the horror that had overpowered him in billowing roars had him weeping with regret. If only he had treated his mother better. If only he hadn't always defied his father. If only he hadn't been so irritated with Rose's questions and Jeremiah's constant trailing of pure adoration.

But it had been too late. Too late for apologies. Too late for his father's forgiveness. Too late to hug his mother and tell her he was sorry. Too late to make up with his siblings and set an example for them to follow. Everything had been too late.

And now as Lemuel Ellis Keagan remembered those days, he felt his heart shrink with chagrin at his behavior. He had been a complete fool. He had lost everyone he'd love most.

All due to his own stupidity.

———

Two months later

"Land ahoy! Land ahoy!" The call shook every sleeping sailor on the ship awake. They rushed here and there, darting this way and that, hollering at each other. Some of the big sails were drawn down slowly but surely. All the sailors obeyed their captain's orders in an organized yet preoccupied manner.

The call heard by the passengers aboard had them all rushing onto the deck to see the land. David spied Elizabeth in the midst of the babbling crowd and edged his way towards her. Grabbing her hand, he laughed at her bewildered expression. "Canada, Beth! Let's go see the Promised Land."

She smiled up at him and then allowed him to pull her along

after him. They made their way through droves of people until they reached the metal railing. Water crashed up against a tall and rocky cliff. Seagulls cried out high above the waters.

"Beth, this is Nova Scotia,"

She squealed. "Nova Scotia? We are going to live here? Oh, it is so beautiful!"

He rolled his eyes. "On the contrary. I have arranged to live in the North West Territories, two hours north of a small mining town called Dawson City."

She looked depressed. "Oh." Her mouth drooped before the girl raised her eyebrows. "Did I just hear you say *'small'* town?"

"Yes, what's wrong with that?"

She sputtered. "Well, I can't live in a small town. I am going to be rich and have servants. How can I be an elegant lady if I live in a small town?"

David snorted. "I think you have the wrong idea here of why I chose to move to Canada. We are moving here for a fresh start, certainly not be rich and prestigious. And I can't understand why you would want to have servants when you had been one your own self! I would think that you would hate to be waited upon, knowing in your heart that you had been one of those poor servants in your past."

She raised her chin, aggravation churning as she heard his reprimanding tone. "I know I previously was an indentured servant but I'm not anymore. Besides, I see no reason why I ought not to be 'waited on'."

The tall man silently appraised her for a long moment. She squirmed beneath his gaze. Finally he spoke and although she disliked what he said, she breathed a sigh of relief. If it was one thing she detested, it was having someone look at her silently without speaking.

"Beth, I thought I already told you that we are not going to have anything such as servants or maids. I do not want that sort of life anymore."

Elizabeth's jaw slackened. "But *why*?!" The words burst out before she could stop them. She bit her lip and sniffed. "Why can't we?"

"Listen to me." David Harrison heaved a sigh. "We are going to become a diligent team who will dedicate ourselves into this new life and are going to surpass any obstacles that threaten to make us fail. I can understand your curiosity in being in control and having people darting here and there for you all the time, but I've experienced it and I hate it! You must learn to think about how *they* feel!"

Elizabeth stared at him, shocked at the vehemence in his tone. His eyes were filled with passion and she swallowed, his words triggering something inside of her heart. He was right and she knew it. She had always hated being treated as a person without emotions or feelings. She had hated being snapped at for accidentally tipping a glass of red wine on the floor. Hated being subjected to as though she were not a person. Yet she hardened her heart against his words.

"I understand what you're saying. I just cannot agree with you. Where you say you want to have a relaxed life is the opposite for me. What I want is to be included in the type of a lifestyle you have just described as unsuitable for your own desires. I *want* to have that life. I would love to be waited upon, hand and foot." She glanced at her own feet, slightly embarrassed. "But I have not a pound to my name. I cannot have that life. Not ever."

The tall man attempted to hide the grin that threatened to protrude from the corners of his mouth as she spoke the words he knew would be coming.

"The only way I could ever have that sort of life is if you would just help me by..." She hesitated, now extremely embarrassed.

He smiled attentively. "What is it?"

She plunged into courage and took off. "Well, I was thinking that perhaps you wouldn't mind to lend me some of your great sums of money so I can have that life." She moistened her dry lips. "I-I know you are rich and since you do not wish for your 'old' life... perhaps you would consider loaning it to me so I can use it for something useful and live my dream?"

He burst out laughing. "Forget it."

Her eyes widened. "I beg your pardon?"

"I said, forget it."

"I heard what you said but I didn't quite believe you had actually meant it."

"I did. And why, Beth?" The tall man's laughter faded. "The truth is that I don't want you to be involved in that life. I don't want you to be waited upon hand and foot. Plainly put, I don't *want* you to be rich."

Tears filled her eyes. "H-how can you even say the words, David? That is the cruelest, most callous, dastardly…the most hateful thing I…" She bit her lip to keep back the flood of tears that threatened to burst the dam.

"How can I say them?" David looked into Elizabeth's eyes. "I say them because I care about you. I do not want you to be in that life because you would become a supercilious, snooty, patronizing Victorian lady. Dressed in silk and lace and reeking the aroma of French perfume, you would become a person I could never even recognize in a few years from now. You have that pompous and conceited character in you already. Can you conceptualize yourself in a few years if you had the opportunity to take all those liberties and become a possible egocentric snob? Beth, under my good conscience I am unable to borrow you any money."

She stared at him, the hurt she had felt only but a few moments before evaporating and transforming into fury. "You are a self-centered lout, David Harrison! A lazy, self-absorbed, self-interested, selfish, and vain boy."

A lazy smile appeared on his lips as though he'd already known she would launch into a tirade. "Perhaps. But you most certainly do use a lot of 'self's' in your vocabulary, don't you? Are you sure you're not referring to yourself?"

She pressed her lips together in outrage. "You proud and cocksure boy! That has nothing to do with what we are discussing."

"Doesn't it?"

They eyed each other for a moment. Challenging. Competing. Daring. Confronting. Disputing through each of their expressions.

She blinked first and happened to glance around herself for one moment. The sight she beheld caused her cheeks to burn. They were drawing unwanted attention unto themselves. The girl flushed with humiliation as she saw people nearby eyeing them and their obvious argument.

The girl gulped and tempered her fury towards the tall man at her side. After all, it would do no good to look like a complete fool in public! Her image would be tainted. Her reputation would be destroyed!

He looked into her deep green eyes and saw that sparks had replaced the tears. She frowned and opened her mouth to respond indignantly but then remembered his words. "Fine, then. Have your way...like usual. Go ahead and be the proud and superior, narrow-minded boy I have always known you to be. It was just that I had begun to think you had perhaps decided to change your ways and become a compassionate, kind fellow. Obviously I was wrong." She narrowed her eyes. "Allow me to assure you that after I turn nineteen, I shall find a way myself. It appears I am not in need for your 'generous' hand in my life after all." She all but snapped out the words.

He raised his eyebrows sardonically. "How remarkable. I wish you success. You're going to need it." At the compressing of her lips and the daggers she shot forth at him, he grinned. Then merely shaking his head, he looked ahead over the ship's railing towards the Promised Land. Canada.

Chapter Eight

A few months later

"**A**re you ready yet?"

Elizabeth stirred, stretching her arms over her head and yawning. Her eyes suddenly flew open, and her heart tripped over itself as she remembered.

"Beth?"

His stern voice reverberating through the door had her gulping. How could she have forgotten the time?! Swallowing hard, the girl bit her lip. "Y-yes?"

The tall man exhaled in frustration. "I certainly hope you are awake by now. It is eight o'clock, and if I recollect correctly, last night we'd determined to leave by seven."

She winced. "Oh, I'm so sorry. I accidentally slept later than I'd intended. I will be right out."

A deep sigh was heard. "All right," he replied shortly. "I'll be waiting by the livery which is just across the street. You can find me there."

She grimaced with irritation as she heard his footsteps disappear down the hall. The man was completely foreign to forgiveness when it came to something that agitated him. Why, he hadn't even accepted her apology!

The rude oaf.

She narrowed her eyes. She ought to have thrown something at the door to express her outrage.

Contrary man.

But then she had been in the wrong, of course. Remorse struck her conscience. She really ought to have forced herself up at six o'clock when she hadn't been able to sleep deeply anyways. But she had given into herself once again when she had snuggled down deeper under the covers in her soft bed. She had taken to constructing a story about a girl who had been a Russian princess until an evil man by the name of Vladimir had stolen the crown from her, making her look and feel like a common pauper! The princess had been thrown out of the castle and onto the streets.

Lying upon the cold ground weak and starving, she would have died had not a kind man by the name of Dmitri Sokolov approached and brought her to his home.

It had taken many months for her to recover. And when she did, Dmitri learned her name was Princess Inessa Kozlov. Of course he did not believe her. How could a commoner be a princess? She was lying, no doubt. After investigating her story, however, Dmitri was shocked to find all the pieces fall in place.

Prince Vladimir was actually not a prince at all! He had greedily wanted the kingdom as his own, and so when the princess's parents had both died, the wicked man had struck gold.

The masquerader had first spoken to the girl's advisors and lawyers, claiming to be the brother of the late king. He'd pointed fingers at Inessa, demanding she be thrown out of the castle. He said she was an interloper, trying to pretend she was the princess.

And he was a good persuader.

The court believed him. The files he had with him forged, of course seemed to prove that he was, indeed, the deceased king's younger brother.

Inessa had been stunned at seeing her 'uncle' for the first time in her life. Upon hearing why he was there, she had tossed all niceties out the window, knowing the fight was on. Arguing that she didn't have any such relative and that her father and mother had been the only children in their families, her protestations were of no avail. The court had remained determined that she was an invader and an intruder pretending to be the princess.

Despite how hard she disputed against the wicked man's words, he had files that 'supported' him and she did not. They had thrown her out and Uncle Vladimir sat upon the throne, head high, mouth twitching in a smug smile.

He had won the battle…again.

Or so he thought.

But then Dmitri took charge. He investigated the story, looked into the background of both Inessa's father and this so-called uncle. The results were flabbergasting.

'Uncle Vladimir' originally came from Germany. Determined to make his fortune in Russia, he'd stoked up a plan that he was sure would catch everyone by surprise. He and his cronies had banded together and with a few tweaks, Vladimir had managed to obtain most of the Russia to believe his lies.

Dmitri pulled some strings and managed to arrange a time to meet the governor. After showing all the proof that Prince Vladimir was actually not a prince at all but a man that belonged in prison a long time ago, the court finally agreed that Princess Inessa had been right.

Although they didn't necessarily say it outright, it was obvious that they knew they had been duped.

Majorly duped.

Princess Inessa took her rightful place back upon the throne and had her lying, thieving 'uncle' sent back to Germany, telling him that if he ever dared to set foot in Russia again she would sentence him to death.

Shortly after, she and Dmitri declared their love for each other. Their eyes were filled with starry benevolence. They had fallen into love, never to fall out of it. Scarcely taking their eyes off of each other, Dmitri Sokolov and Inessa Kozlov were married in May becoming Mr. and Mrs. Dmitri.

And as most fairy tale stories Elizabeth made up ended, they lived happily ever after.

The end.

At least that was the end of her imaginary story. Her *own* story did not end so happily, however.

She had her own share of troubles. *Almost like Princess Inessa,* she thought dreamily, her mind going off to 'Storyland' again. She shook her head as though to rid of the entertaining account spun in her fantasies. Her mind turned and redirected its course back to David Harrison.

The hateful man, she fumed. *The very least he could have done was to acknowledge my apology.*

He was a rude, insensitive man who did not care a thing about her or anyone else. Except himself.

At least that was what she thought of him. She hadn't meant to sleep in, but wasn't it exactly like him to think she had done it intentionally?

Still frustrated, she packed her valise and made up the bed. Leaving the room just as she'd entered it the previous evening, the girl descended down the stairs. She marched confidently across the dusty street to the livery, remembering their journey to the province of Ontario.

They had left Nova Scotia nearly a month ago and had taken the Intercolonial Railway from there to Ontario. Elizabeth had enjoyed the luxurious train ride. The scenery rattling by the squealing blur of the train was also incredible. She had only been in a carriage but a few times in her entire life, and the experience surpassed any ideas she had entertained of high class society. She felt as though she could have ridden on that train for the rest of her life!

Bringing her thoughts back home, she walked into the stable looking for David. But no David was to be seen. Where was he?

"Lookin' for somethin', miss? If you are, I think you've found the wrong place. We don't take kindly to horse thieves here in Cornwall."

Elizabeth whirled around to see a huge blacksmith staring at her suspiciously. The man was one of the biggest men she'd ever beheld.

Muscles bulged from under his loose, threadbare jacket. His right hand sported a red hot poker, and his eyes glared at her menacingly. Anger tore at her but she just managed to control her tongue before she blurted out something she was sure she'd regret.

Elizabeth involuntarily took a step back. She gaped at his discourteous manner. "Uh, no. I'm…" She stuttered, feeling stunned at his words. She was a genteel lady and he didn't have any right to point a finger at her.

"I am looking for my husband, sir." The burning fire of humiliation spread over her cheeks but she refused to take acknowledgement of it. After all, this boorish barbarian had no right to speak to her in such outrageously rude behavior. "H-His name is David Harrison. He's particularly tall with black hair and blue eyes. If you are looking for precise measurements, he is approximately six feet, five inches. I believe he was here earlier, acquiring two horses."

He stared at her, the suspicion slowly evaporating.

"David Harrison? Ah, yes, I know the man." He saw her blush and apparently misunderstood the cause for it. "You must be newlyweds."

The girl's cheeks turned a deeper shade of crimson. The big man grinned. "All right. He's just…" He suddenly frowned. "Ain't you a bit young to be married?"

Her heart sank. This was the end of her act. After all, if she told him she sixteen he might still take her as a horse thief and as a liar!

There was only one last thing to do.

And that was to lie again.

She forced her eyes to widen. "I'm eighteen, sir," she replied, trying to sound nonchalant.

He shook his head, baffled. "You sure look young for your age."

She drew a shaky breath. "Yes, many people inform me of that. I suppose it's a blessing." She offered a weak grin.

She breathed a sigh of relief when the man appeared to believe her whopping lie. "Please forgive me, Mrs. Harrison. I sure never intended to greet you to Cornwall this way. Your husband's filled me in on where you're headed." He stuck out his grimy blackened hand and smiled extensively.

Elizabeth didn't quite dare to shake it but in fear that she might anger him if she didn't, she politely shook it in return. The blacksmith's hand was harder than a rock with all his thick calluses. She tried not to cry out in pain as the man's gigantic paw swallowed her hand and shook it profusely, squeezing too hard.

Elizabeth tried to smile but had the feeling it came out more like a grimace. "Of course, sir, and it is a pleasure to make your acquaintance."

After the hand squeeze instead of a handshake the blacksmith said, "Your husband is out that back door over there behind the livery, waiting..." A thought struck him. "You must be the one he's waiting for."

She wanted to holler in his doltish face, "Well, obviously! How stupid are you, anyways?" But she had enough common sense to realize she didn't want to be on the wrong side of this man.

After pointing the way, he added, "The trek out North is a long and hard one. I hear only the strong survive. Your husband told me you folks are headed onto the North West Territories. I wish you all the luck for your trip." He paused. "Be grateful that you're traveling during the summer as that'll help you prepare for the rough winter."

She nodded, attempting to look grateful for the advice. "Thank you, sir. I'll remember your words of wisdom."

She walked through the door he had pointed to, softly adjuring that this would be the last time she'd ever meet anyone quite as big and menacing as that blacksmith.

———

Elizabeth squinted as the bright sunlight outside momentarily blinded her. As her eyes adjusted, she saw David before her with two large horses on either side of him. One was charcoal black and the other a deep chestnut.

Elizabeth looked at him and remembered the lie she had just spoken. She bit her lip anxiously.

"You're finally here," he glowered. "Did something occur to have caused this delay?"

He barks the words as though I am a dog, she thought rather indignantly. The girl cleared her throat, deciding to ignore his impatient words. She didn't suppose she had really ever spoken a lie in her entire life and this one was eating her up. "David, I did something wrong. I've just lied to that blacksmith."

His expression darkened. "About what?"

"I-I said that you were my husband. He acted as though I were a horse thief and because I was afraid he would throw me straight into a dirty jail cell, I told him that you were my husband."

At first the tall man just stared at her but then he burst out laughing.

She glared at him, totally oblivious to what was so amusing. "Well, I didn't want to be hung!"

David's laughter slowly faded. "I admire your spunk. I also think it'd be a good idea to tell everyone that we're married."

She sighed in exasperation. "Why?"

"There may be outlaws and vagabonds on our journey north and I do not want you to get into a dire situation."

She nodded slowly, although clearly confused by his words. He decided it was time for a change in the subject.

"What do you think of them?" he asked as he stroked the calm beasts by his side, apparently wanting her opinion.

Elizabeth looked at the animals in awe. Their mossy brown eyes of liquid blinked. And when Elizabeth gazed into their gentle eyes, she felt she was looking straight into their hearts. Their sleek and shiny coats looked unbelievably smooth and Elizabeth could not resist reaching out and touching both of the horses' faces. "They are beautiful," she breathed.

He nodded, pleased by her enthusiasm. "These horses are Morgans which were first discovered in 1792. The breed received

62

their name from a man by the name of Justin Morgan. From what the blacksmith told me, this breed has a reputation for intelligence, courage, and an easy disposition." He paused before adding, "This is Black." David rested a palm on the big horse's neck.

Elizabeth made a face. "Black? Seriously, David, how original. Why not consider calling him something more solicitous?" She tipped her head, thinking. "I've got it!" she exclaimed, snapping her fingers. "We can call him Braveheart."

The tall man shook his head at her, smiling. "Though I don't see what difference it makes, Braveheart it is."

The girl clasped her hands together and beamed. "What is the chestnut's name?"

David grinned. "I thought you could do the honors as she is to be your mount. That is, if you can think of a name that suits her. Otherwise we'll just commence calling her Chestnut."

"Wildfire," she said, her expression dreamy. "Her name is Wildfire."

North West Territories, Canada

He brushed away the moisture in his eyes, his heart squeezing with pain. The memory hurt.

He'd woken up by perhaps his instinct that something was wrong and had immediately turned to glance at his grandson on his lap. He was relieved to see the lad had been sleeping. Then he turned to look at his daughter. He'd been startled to see her eyes fixed upon him. "Livie, you're awake!" he exclaimed joyously. "You're goin' to get well now."

His daughter had shaken her head slowly. He could see she was weak. "No, Papa," she whispered, her throat sounding parched. "I am awake, yes, but I am not going to become well. Of that I am sorry."

Her words brought a feeling of horror and denial transfixed through him. "You don't know what you're sayin'! Of course you are a goin' to get well. You just feel mighty weak right now but by tomorrow you'll be on the mend." His heart constricted when she slowly shook her head.

"I love you. Thank you for being my father." She blinked away the tears that threatened to fall. "You are the closest and the most special person to me next to Rankin and Keith, of course."

Lemuel's heart cracked. "Olivia...don't go! Don't leave me!" he pleaded, his voice taking on a desperate tone. But the woman had smiled softly and then she closed her eyes leaving her father and son on earth alone.

The old man remembered covering his daughter's body because the earth was to frozen to dig a grave. His young grandson had stood beside him staring wide-eyed. Later in the spring he had dug a grave and lowered the homemade wooden coffin silently.

"Mama?" the boy had questioned, glancing up at his grandfather and then down at the grave.

"Yes, Keith," the old man said gravely. "Your mother is gone away to a different world."

Picking up the tearful little boy, Lemuel had begun to walk back to the cabin. Their lives had forever been changed.

And now as Lemuel thought about that sad day, he felt his heart pang. How much he missed Olivia. She had caused his bleak-looking life to become a shining star. A brightened world. But that happiness had disappeared. Death has taken it from him. Oh, how he missed Olivia!

Chapter Nine

"David, do you remember my mother?"

The tall man turned to her. "Yes. Don't you?"

She sighed. "Well, slightly. It is just that she passed away when I had been such a young age, and I find myself forgetting her sometimes."

"I see."

They maneuvered their horses silently down a steep, narrow portion of the trail. But when the going was level, David still did not answer.

The girl frowned. "Can you please answer my question?"

He started in the saddle. "I apologize. I was thinking about something else for a moment."

She flashed him a look of annoyance. "Obviously."

"Of course," he replied pleasantly. "Well, one of the things I can recall is that she had your speech and character more than your looks. Your looks must be mostly contributed to your grandparents. What did they look like?"

He inwardly grimaced. Talking to her was like trying to walk on a bed of nails. Everything he said had to be thought over as quickly as possible before he spoke the words.

The girl frowned slightly. "Now that you mention it, I have actually never heard anything of my grandparents. If my memory can serve correctly, not once did my mother or father ever discuss their own parents. I cannot help but wonder if I have any! Do you recollect my parents ever mentioning them?"

The tall man burst out laughing at her innocent conclusions. "Beth, of course you have grandparents! Every person has two sets of grandparents, and it is obvious that you do as well."

She frowned. "No, I didn't mean it that way. I meant that perhaps my mother was an orphan and has not a single parent she can recall."

David eyed her with mirth. "You sound as though you are enjoying the very thought of that. Why would you think of your mother that way?"

"If I should never know, what is there to deter me from imagining where she might have come from? What I mean is, why should I have to be locked in a jail with bars all around me? That is a figure of speech I once read it in a book and I found it so enchanting that I use it whenever an opportunity arises. I find it extremely fascinating to imagine…"

She gasped. "I just thought of something divine. What if my grandmother was a really rich lady who had lived in the biggest castle the world has ever known? What if I have royal blood in me?" She turned eager eyes to her guardian. "Could you imagine if you are actually riding beside the long lost granddaughter of a royal personage? Can you imagine if I were really the richest lady on earth? And what about gold coins and silver dollars? Consider the implication if I am being searched for through all of England so I can be restored to my former glory! But of course," she finished with a sigh, "no longer am I in England, so I suppose that illusion is lost and is now all in vain of any hope for rescue."

David turned his head, his shoulders shaking slightly.

Elizabeth continued rambling on.

"Oh, but what if word has escaped to the ears of a really wicked man who is determined to have my hand in marriage so as to become the possessor of all my worldly goods?"

She was talking to herself now, her green eyes taking on a

faraway look. They widened at the notable extraordinary fantasies she envisioned. As she rambled on, David could see a new side to Elizabeth. It was a side he had seldom, if ever, gotten a glimpse of.

"After he cajoles me into joining the marital life with him, he is already making preparations to murder me in my sleep! The wretched man is developing ideas of how to murder me with a rope to make it look as though I had actually committed suicide all by myself. And he is even scheming to hide my dead body behind the churchyard by the gravestones of two extremely evil men to look as though I had been in cahoots with them!"

David was having a difficult time keeping back the laughter that was nearly choking him. "Beth," he finally managed. "Are you okay?"

The girl jumped as though she'd been stung by a bee. "What?" she screeched in shock, her head swiveling around.

"Were you telling yourself a story?" The tall man couldn't resist teasing her.

She stuttered. "Uh…I must have forgotten who I was talking to."

He saw she was embarrassed and attempted to reassure her. "Well, I think you are a natural storyteller. Your narration had me transfixed with attentiveness."

She beamed. "Really?"

"Really." He chuckled at the breathless expression that had lit upon her features.

"That's nice, because if you don't mind I am going to continue with it."

His smile grew at her dreamy tone. "All right, and I shall be your audience," he joked.

She was already back into her dramatic mesmeric, thus it appeared she hadn't even heard him. Gazing off to the distant horizon, she smiled. The girl's face was glowing in a flickering light of a dreamy fantasy. She was away in her world of make-belief and fairy tales.

"My hateful husband was determined to take my gold so he

decided to murder and kill me. He did not realize, however, that a secret admirer from when I had been young had overheard him and his cronies talking…"

David sheltered a sigh. It was going to be a long ride.

———

North West Territories, Canada

It had never been discussed, but in each man's heart they knew what they were doing: taking something that didn't belong to them.

Coveting. Stealing. Lying. Murdering.

Thousands of thoughts had flitted through Lemuel's mind as he remembered the years of his growing up. *Thou shalt not steal. Thou shalt not covet. Thou shalt not kill…* The words haunted him. They had haunted his mind almost night and day.

But he'd forced them away.

He hadn't wanted to be reminded of the wrong he had been doing. The wrong his mother had told him about in his childhood. He hadn't wanted to remember all that his mother had taught him in his childhood. He'd wanted to forget that all. But he couldn't. And deep down inside of him, he knew it would never leave him. *Proverbs 22: 6. Train up a child in the way he should go: and when he is old, he will not depart from it.*

Discouraged with the way his life had turned out, the tall wizened man shrugged his deflated shoulders and decided he couldn't change it anymore. His life was the way it was. But the thing he did forget was that there was One who could change it. One who *he* had forgotten, but One who had not forgotten him.

———

"Mama, why did you have to go and leave me alone?"

"Beth. You're having a nightmare."

Elizabeth opened her eyes and blinked. It was midnight; nearby

68

an owl hooted. The clouds were melting into each other like ice cream beneath the summer sun, and the moonlight lit up the night with a sparkling radiance. Elizabeth shivered. As she lifted her hand to rub her eyes, she suddenly felt tears and knew she had been crying in her sleep.

"Are you all right?" It was David.

She looked across the flickering firelight at him only able to see his face's outline as the fire's shadows danced across his features.

"I was dreaming about my…"

"About your mother," David supplied quietly.

She nodded. "Yes. I was dreaming about…" Tears filled her eyes and she could say no more.

"Shhh. Just go back to sleep, okay? Everything will look brighter in the morning."

She nodded silently, a sense of security flooding her. At least David was here. He would keep her safe, wouldn't he?

The girl tried to sleep. She tossed and turned for a while before eventually giving up. Elizabeth lay there, thinking about those days when her mother had still been alive. She thought about when she'd had those cozy nights with her mother in their little cottage far of in England.

Everything about her childhood was gone. All there that was left was her future. The darkening doom of her future stretched ahead of her in a long, straight road. That was all. She was alone in a strange country and equally unknown land. She was really just an urchin; that was all she was. A poor, miserable street urchin. A useless waif.

Tears squeezed their way out of her closed eyelids and then trickled down both sides of her cheeks. Why had she ever thought anything could be different?

No, nothing has changed, nor will it ever. I am bound for a life of disappointment and tears.

Still weeping, she fell into a fitful sleep. She entered a strange dream.

She was walking down a path of golden stones. There must have been a lot of lights as everything was bright, but when the girl looked up she could not find a single one. Everything was a vibrant gold. Such heavenly golden light! Golden castles arose high into the sky, superior and regal. White clad figures walked near the castles on the paved paths. Sometimes they flew high in the brilliant sky above. Many had wings so white they hurt her eyes and Elizabeth had to squint to be able to see.

She continued walking in complete awe. The lighting became brighter and brighter. She was intrigued by the pure celestial vision. And then quite suddenly she came upon a narrow gate. She stood there, stupefied. Suddenly a hand appeared out of nowhere and beckoned for her to enter. The gate began to open slowly, perhaps by its own accord. Beyond the gate, Elizabeth captured a glimpse of even whiter golden beauty. But then she could not bear to look any longer. She had to look away for the golden light was too bright for her earthly eyes.

She tried to locate the "Person" whose hand was calling her to enter but all she could see was a perfect hand stretched out, continually waving for her to enter into the open gate. As she was about to take a step forwards, something held her back. She hesitated. And then something within her hardened her heart. She stiffened. Turning on one heel, she whirled and ran away from the angelic almost heavenly beauty. As she turned around to see one more glance at the beauty, she saw a golden angel standing there just watching her.

Resentment smote her heart. She increased her pace, gasping for breath. But as she ran, the world around her darkened. The beautiful golden light she had seen was transpiring into an obscure background. She turned back around, squinting, trying to find the golden bright beauty. But it had disappeared.

Suddenly a small ugly form of a serpent arose from out of nowhere. He hissed at her, his cold eyes narrowing as he began to speak. "Lost, are you?" he wheezed. "I can help you. Just follow me. Follow me. The place I am going has such warmth. Oh, such warmth." He cackled an evil laugh.

Elizabeth shivered. She shook her head, glancing behind her towards the mysterious golden gate then back at the wicked snake. The girl opened her mouth to scream but at that moment she awoke in cold sweat.

It was only a dream. She forced herself to believe that.

Why then was her heart so heavy with troubled thoughts? Why was she so afraid?

It was a long time before she fell back asleep.

———

The bright sun shone down on Elizabeth, causing her to squirm. She opened her eyes and blinked, trying to adjust her vision to the brightness of the sun.

As she remembered the previous night, she felt a jolt of pain stab her soul.

Why do I always have to think about things that make me feel sad? she wondered. *Some people just have a tragic life. I can't change that. Nobody can.*

As another thought shot through her head like a stray bullet, she forced herself to ignore it. *God? What can He do?* She scoffed inwardly. *He doesn't do anything except favor certain people over others. I'm just "homely, scrawny Elizabeth Davison way in Canada who was formerly a serving girl."*

Her mother had always told Elizabeth about the Lord, but now all those times in their small cottage far off in England seemed to vanish.

If there even is a God, she thought bitterly, *I doubt He has enough time to even remember me. After all, I don't come from a prestigious background. My heritage is like a damper on my life. Why did I have to be born into a poor family? It's not that I don't love my parents, but...*

if only they could have been born into a royal heritage! I'd be rich, respected and popular.

Brushing away the thoughts, she attempted to forget them. After all, her life was the way it was. She couldn't change it. The God she scarcely believed in couldn't change it. *He'd* made that very clear to her, or so she thought.

Her life was destined for disaster. And that was the end of the subject.

Chapter Ten

North West Territories, Canada

He had forbidden that his daughter's name be spoken in the cabin at all. Keith knew the silent rules that Lemuel kept and obeyed them. Olivia was never talked about. Everything was kept silent; silent in their own lonely, broken hearts of both affliction and longing.

Oh, Lemuel loved his grandson. He'd drummed survival as the key word to living in this wild land. The young boy knew nearly as much about wilderness living as did his grandfather. Lemuel Ellis Keagan had taught his grandson well. At least he could be given credit for that.

Training; patient training. He had worked hard preparing the boy for life out in the wilderness. Even before Keith was old enough to talk, Ellis Keagan had shown the young lad the plants that were dangerous and the plants that were medicinal. As Keith grew, Lemuel had taught him firearm safety and had vehemently stated that firearms were not a toy and that they were a weapon.

The old man had refused to tell his grandson that he'd formerly squeezed the trigger as he aimed at people's hearts without a thought of remorse. He'd killed people.

The thought of what he was really doing never penetrated into his mind. Being an outlaw was his life. And shooting, killing, stealing, lying…it had all been a part of it.

Lemuel had forced his thoughts away from that area of his life. Instead of dwelling on his dark past, he had spent as much time as possible with his grandson.

The young boy was bright. At the age of four, he had been able to safely handle the .22 rifle. One day he had shot a hawk that was threatening to take off with one of their few chickens. It was a remarkable shot for a boy of his age!

Ah yes, Lemuel loved his grandson. In his heart, though, he knew that leaving the young boy at the cabin for days at a time while he went out to check his traps was nothing short of unnerving.

During those long winter treks, Lemuel would often think about the boy and wonder how he was coping.

Especially when it got down to a raw minus forty degrees out, a bundle of nerves had never left his heart after taking that first step away from the cabin. Until he returned, the constant fear that something might have happened to Keith would not leave his heart. His grandson was the only relative he had left on this earth was Keith.

Olivia had not been his biological daughter. No, at one point she had been nothing short of a homeless child wandering the streets. Lemuel had come upon her one late afternoon in the town of Dawson City. Her small, scrawny form and frightened doe-like eyes had drawn him to her and with that first step, he had unknowingly taken her into his heart as well.

Despite the fact that he did not know a farthing's worth of her parents or background, Lemuel had loved the girl as his own daughter. And she had returned the love. Nothing had ever really been spoken about her unofficial adoption so Lemuel suspected her husband Rankin hadn't even known. They had lived their lives together in their wilderness. They had lived and laughed together and Lemuel had nearly felt happy.

But not quite.

His past was a damper upon his soul.

Olivia had never noticed anything out of the ordinary from

his actions. She had always adored him beyond adoration. Lemuel wished he could tell her all the wrongs he had done. All the faults he still had. He didn't like the look of wonder and almost worship that had wreathed the girl's face. He hadn't wanted her to exalt him into near reverence. He wanted to tell her all the wrongs he had done. He wanted to tell her that he was nothing to idolize.

But he refrained, knowing her conscience was too pure and innocent for her to carry the load that her adopted father was an outlaw. Had been an outlaw for the past thirty years! Lemuel had kept that secret hidden from her.

She had never guessed the truth.

But oh, how Lemuel wished for Olivia to return to him.

————

One month later

"England, eh?" Beady eyes scrutinized the two standing in front of his desk. "Humph." The land broker of True North Domain shook his head. "Never been there. Although there are many of the English in this country, not many are up in this part of Canada." The man pointed to the map laid out on his desk with his pudgy finger.

Elizabeth watched as David leaned forwards to examine the map more closely. The broker caught on to David's interest. He spoke quickly, not wanting to lose a good sale.

"Well, this should do just fine. I do have other parcels of land if that might interest you, some of them bigger than the one mentioned, some slightly smaller. But in my opinion, I think you should start out small and grow big. With just you and your wife, a hundred and sixty acres would do good. For starters, anyway."

"That much? That is a lot, sir!" Elizabeth squeaked suddenly. The broker and David both turned and stared at her. "Well, shouldn't we first begin with a smaller acreage?" She was embarrassed now and shifted eyes to David. Judging from his glare it was obvious he was irked she had interrupted.

"Be quiet, Beth," David snapped.

She looked down at the rough floorboards of the little room, a slight blush beginning to form on her prominent cheekbones. "On second thought, I confess I do not know much about this particular field. I apologize for interfering." The girl could not seem to hide the infuriating reddening upon her cheekbones which partially contributed to both discomposure and chagrin at David's brusque words.

The broker seemed nonchalant. "Oh, don't you worry none about it, ma'am," he exclaimed cheerfully. "It's good to ask questions. That's how you learn, ain't it?" He chuckled and then spat onto the floor, mere inches from her boot.

Elizabeth was extremely insulted. Despite her irritation towards the man, however, she drew every ounce of fortitude and forced her lips to form a sweet smile. "Thank you for being so understanding, sir," she answered cordially.

The two men didn't even notice her after that. They were too busy arguing over what the price should be. Elizabeth sighed. Would she have to sit here all afternoon?

It was just then that the broker's voice rose higher into almost a mouse piercing squeak as he protested against what David had just uttered. Elizabeth jerked up her head and looked at the individuals with wide eyes. Why was the broker shouting?

David Harrison grinned that slow, mechanical grin. He stretched out his long legs in front of him, crossing them at the ankles. "I named the price I think it's worth," he commented calmly. "If you don't accept my offer, we'll just go to the North West Land Quest across the street."

The broker's eyes were prodigious. He gawked at David. There was a long, awkward silence. Finally he spoke. "You drive a hard bargain, Harrison, but I'm willing to do it for…" He hesitated then spoke such a price that Elizabeth practically fell from her chair from shock.

David quirked an eyebrow. "I guess you didn't understand what I meant." He stood up, beckoning for Elizabeth to also rise. "See you around." He acknowledged the broker before he began to stride purposely away.

The little man jumped off his chair and scurried around the desk.

"Now, now, there ain't no need for you to go off runnin' in a huff just because you didn't get your price." He managed to snag David's sleeve with his corpulent fingers.

The tall man eyed the broker strangely. "I'm not running off in a huff because I didn't get what I asked," he mimicked almost sarcastically.

The little man let out a nervous guffaw. "Sure wasn't my intent to offend you," he backtracked. "In fact, I…I was just seein' how you would react."

David just contemplated the man. "Is that so?" Then he turned and continued his walk towards the door.

The little man hopped after him. "Wait, mister. I've changed my mind. You have such a fetching wife," he crooned, "that I'm willin' to give it for your offer. You see, it ain't often that we get such a pretty lady come into town."

Elizabeth felt her mouth go dry. She was so flattered by his words! Even if they did come from *him*.

"And I ain't meaning any disrespect to you at all, ma'am," the man added.

Elizabeth was radiant. However, after sneaking her 'husband' a few hesitant glances, David saw she attempted to rein in her elation. "Oh, there certainly isn't any offense taken on my account, sir." She smiled rather stiffly as she saw David's eyes narrow at her ecstatic response. "Well, at least not in this instance," she added somewhat reluctantly.

The broker let out a sigh of relief, also eying David with slight perturbation. "Thank you kindly." He fiddled with his fingers nervously, awaiting David's response. Was it too late now? But oh how he did not want his rival across the street to get this customer. After all, this tall man had offered a price that was nearly foreign to him!

David thought a moment then shook his head. "No, I still think I'll go check it out by North West. Perhaps I will receive a more 'diverting' offer."

The broker thought he would die of mortification if he would have to hear Scott Morrisey bragging to everyone at the saloon tonight about how much money he had procured from a rich immigrant who had purchased a parcel of land off him.

He made a quick decision. After all, his honor and reputation was at stake.

"All right, all right," he grumbled. Then he proclaimed a price low enough that was obviously a factor in making David pause, turn around, and consider. His gaze met Elizabeth's. She bit her lip, uncertain of what to say.

The broker pivoted pleading eyes upon her. "Can't you persuade him, miss?"

Elizabeth just offered a tentative smile. She disliked it immensely when David upbraided her in public when she offered an opinion or suggestion. But the broker continued. "After all, this is to be your home too. And I'm tellin' you, girl. The soil is deep and dark. You can grow the biggest garden this side of Dawson with all them pretty flowers around your home. Imagine folks comin' from miles around just to ask about your secrets and to capture but a glimpse of your pretty face. I wouldn't doubt that folks will be under such a spell that they'll take to callin' you the Queen of Flowers."

Elizabeth was always one to fall prey to a beautiful fantasy, and this man had the ability to speak words like poetry. She gushed over the idea of being popular. Besides, the man had just complimented her on her hair. She felt such appreciation towards him that she brightened immediately. Forgetting her fear of David publicly embarrassing her, she spoke up.

"Oh, please, David! Don't be such a stick in the mud." She sashayed for one moment, the perfect coy wife. "If you don't purchase it, I'll forever be miserable. And you wouldn't want that now, would you?"

The broker watched in glee as the girl worked her magic on her husband. She was perfect! Oh, surely he would get a sale now!

She tugged on his sleeve. "If you really love me, you will do this for me." She batted her lashes in mock impertinence. "You do love me, don't you?"

Chapter Eleven

David shook his head, grinning. This girl was full of surprises. How did she pull it off anyways? She looked totally real…if he wouldn't have known her better.

He sighed and grinned, deciding to go along with her game. "All right, darling. I'll get it for you. But you have to promise to make me one of your delicious dinners with chicken and dumplings."

He watched in amusement as Elizabeth's smile diminished in size. She knew he was teasing her. But then she lit up, and the act was on once again.

"Of course, dearest Davey. I would do anything for you." Sarcasm, David thought. Well, two could play the game.

"Indeed," the man said wryly. He suddenly appeared to realize what she'd just called him. His jaw tightened. "And sweetheart," he gritted. "Please don't call me that."

Elizabeth smiled impishly. Her eyes shone with mischief. "Call you what, Davey?"

The tall man shot her a hard look of irritation. "You know what I mean."

Elizabeth cocked her head, absently fingering a long red curl. "Do I?"

The broker felt panic flood through him. Thanks to that girl he had nearly achieved a sale. But now she was attempting to create havoc with her words? If she angered his client too much, the man had no doubts that David Harrison would march straight out the door.

He had to stop them!

"Now, missy," he blurted. "I don't think your husband likes it when you commence to callin' him 'Davey'."

Elizabeth whirled on him, green eyes flashing. "Oh, really? Well, he always calls me 'Beth' and that is also aggravating! I figure he deserves to receive a shortened version of his name as well. In fact, I'm doing it just to spite him."

The tall man's jaw clenched with anger. She was making a fool out of the both of them.

The broker's mouth dropped. "Y-you mean you are *deliberately* angering your husband?" he asked incredulously. "But…it ain't right to anger him!"

Elizabeth's stared in surprise. "Right? What is not right about it? He's always calling me by 'Beth'. Don't you think that is rude as well?"

The broker could not reply. He merely gawked at the fiery redhead.

Then spinning upon David again, the girl narrowed her eyes. "If you tell me why you never call me by my full name, I will stop calling you 'Davey'."

David tightened his lips and grasped both her shoulders within a firm grip. "No, you will stop right now at this present instant. Do you understand?"

Elizabeth stared at him, dumbfounded. Then anger set in again. She glowered at him before her facade of iron wore off. "But *why* must you call me 'Beth'?" she asked in a plaintive tone. "My name is *Elizabeth!*"

"The reason is personal," he bit out. "Now, you will never call me by 'Davey' again or you will receive such a punishment you won't know what hit you."

Her eyes filled with tears at his harsh tone. "Are you insinuating that you would" she glanced around meaningfully then whispered hoarsely "*beat* me if I wouldn't stop?"

David shook his head. "No, of course not! But I will certainly punish you another way. And believe me, you wouldn't like it." Actually, the tall man hadn't an idea of what type of punishment he would give her, but his threat appeared to have been successful for the girl swallowed hard.

"I-I'm sorry for provoking you."

David suddenly surprised her by giving her an impish grin. He released her shoulders. "Don't ever do that again and I forgive you."

"I promise I won't," she replied.

David squeezed her hand before turning to the broker who was rubbing his hands together in anticipation. "Well?" he demanded. "You heard my wife. Don't I have some paperwork to sign?"

The broker started. "Uh…yes." He shook his head and offered his most cordial smile before returning to his rightful place behind the desk.

David and Elizabeth also resumed their uncomfortable seats.

While the broker reached into his desk and drew out two pages, David pulled out an enormous pile of money from his pocket. She gawked openly at the huge stack. Enviously. The tall man counted out the total bills and handed it over to the broker who was so greedy that when he snatched the money from David's hand he practically ripped the bills into half!

Elizabeth bit back a giggle. David nudged her to silence while he took the offered paper, filled in all the required information and put his signature beside the X. The broker wrote his signature which was actually a scrawl and proffered one of the small white papers to David. The tall man tucked it neatly into his vest.

Then the men shook hands.

"Thank you, Harrison. You too, ma'am." He gave her an ear-splitting grin before his expression sobered as he added, "Many come, not many stay."

David looked across at Elizabeth and took her hand. "We'll

stay," he said as he smiled down at her. Elizabeth returned his smile, happiness surging throughout her soul.

The broker looked at their expectant faces and sadly shook his head. "That's what they all say," he sighed.

David just smiled.

———

David and Elizabeth walked down the dusty streets of Dawson City. The tall man grinned down at her. "I'm thinking of going out to the blacksmith's and look around for some horses that would be good for working the land."

Elizabeth nodded. "All right, I'll just go browse around this town."

David gave her a puzzled look. "Aren't you coming with me?"

"No," she shook her head. "I would enjoy seeing what is really in this wild and dusty town of Dawson City."

The tall man shrugged. "Fine with me. Let's meet in front of the general store when we're finished," he suggested.

"All right," she smiled.

For a moment she stood there watching David stride purposely towards the blacksmith shop. Elizabeth fanned herself as the sun beat down unmercifully upon her head. As she gazed about herself, she saw men riding past her on horseback, often tipping their Stetsons in respect towards her, their spurs flashing in the sun's rays. It caught the girl's attention that each man had a gun belt strapped to his thigh at all times. The pistol handles glared at her from their holsters, and Elizabeth shivered. What a murderous, demon-possessed weapon! Little did she know that she would behold more handguns in the upcoming days.

She heard the twinkling tune of the piano nearby and frowned. A piano? She glanced about herself until she espied a building to her left with a large wooden plank tacked to the door. *Lucky Devil's Saloon was* written on it in large letters.

Elizabeth's expression transformed to interest. A saloon? The respectable people had said that saloons were nefarious. But…what were they really like inside? Curiosity got the better of her, and Elizabeth marched up to the large billiard with its flat false front and wide boardwalk flanking the dusty street. Upon reaching it, she bit her lower lip. Uncertain. Should she go inside?

She threw back her shoulders. It was a challenge.

The girl strode right in, the swinging doors brushing against her dress. What a sight met her amazing eyes!

The room was begrimed and grungy with the distasteful odor of smoke infiltrating the air. It was loud inside. Loud and boisterous. She gazed about the room, taking in everything with unabashed interest.

The long paneled mahogany bar was polished until it gleamed as the dim lights cast their shadows across the otherwise dust-covered room. Skirting the plinth of the bar was a smooth brass foot rail as well as tall round stools which a man could sit on to knock back his glass of bourbon or beer. Tall shelves covered the entire wall behind the bar, reaching from the floor to the ceiling. Bottles and glasses of various shapes and sizes were scattered across them. Men slouched at round tables with green covers smoking cigars or chewing tobacco while playing or dealing cards. There was also a long pool table that stood near the back of the room where approximately half a dozen men stood around talking while taking turns to shoot the balls home with their cue sticks.

The jaunty tune of the piano in the background now irritated her. She drew a deep breath but accidentally inhaled too much smoke and began to cough. A few dozen heads pivoted her way. She blushed, embarrassed.

One man in particular pushed back his chair and stood up. Elizabeth blinked in surprise as he approached her.

"Well, what do we have here?" he asked, a strange gleam in his eyes. He reached out and grasped an auburn curl.

Elizabeth's jaw promptly dropped in disbelief as he twirled it around his dirty finger. "Wh-whatever are you doing, sir?" she finally managed.

He chuckled. "And she even calls me 'sir'! Oh, I like that."

A cacophony of racketing laughter joined him as the entire saloon watched the scene unfold before them.

Elizabeth appraised the man for a moment. He was of medium height and probably in his mid-twenties. His clothing was in rough disrepair, and his black hair reached his shoulders. He had apparently not shaven in a while for his cheeks were covered in rough stubble. Elizabeth wrinkled her nose at the bodily odor he proffered and endeavored to stifle her repulsion towards him.

"Missy, you're one pretty gal," the man said.

She tried to smile at the compliment but something seemed strange about the atmosphere in the room. It was almost eerie, she thought. The piano playing had ceased and now the room contained silence. A frightening silence.

The man frowned slightly. "Ain't you gonna tell us your business here?" When she didn't answer, he grasped her arm tightly within his clutch. "Well, missy, it's time you learn that when I ask you a question, you answer."

Elizabeth winced as his fingers dug into her flesh. She frowned, trying to twist her arm out of his grip. "If you want me to speak, then I demand for you to release my arm at once!"

A low rumble erupted from his throat. "I think not. You'll speak the way you are."

Irritation flooded her. "I beg your pardon?" she shrieked. "Are you insinuating that I am to be held with violence as a low-down criminal in a free country? Because if you think I'm some female wimp who will succumb to all your orders, you can think again! I stand upon my own two feet, and I will most assuredly not be told what to do by a dirty man! Thank you very much."

Her response was met with silence. The men looked stunned by her admission. The girl lifted her chin. "And just to clarify, I assure you that I am not jesting. Release me at once or I shall call the police immediately. I will claim that you have been manhandling me. Which, at present, you are." She turned her gaze to address the crowd. "Since you are such disagreeable, rude people, I will not hesitate to remain here but a minute longer." With that spoken, Elizabeth turned on one heal and began to march out. She had forgotten that the man still had her arm grasped within his fingers for she was yanked unceremoniously back to the disagreeable man. Turning, she glared at him. "You odious beast. Unhand me this minute, I say!"

"I already said I ain't gonna do it. You are goin' to have to make me." He grinned, certain that this female (like so many others) would not be able to.

He was mistaken.

Elizabeth drew her lips in a straight line of resentment. She narrowed her eyes and jerked her foot back. She then kicked the man in his shin as hard as she possibly could. In fact, she had kicked him so hard that the force nearly knocked her backwards. She stumbled and then crashed into another man. He looked startled for a moment, then after receiving a nod from the man she had just kicked, the wretched bloke grabbed her wrist with his hand.

She opened her mouth to retort her outrage, but the man growled in her ear. "Girl, you best behave yourself if you know what's good for you. Nobody does that to the Fox without gettin' their payback."

The man, presumably called Fox, once again strode purposely towards her, limping only slightly.

Elizabeth's throat was now dry with terror as he reached her side once again. She struggled against the other man's tight grip. "You snake!" she cried. "You wicked snake!"

"You callin' me a snake, girly?" He gave her an oily smile. "Well, I've been called many other names but I don't suppose I ain't ever been called that before."

Elizabeth was wild with fear. As the Fox snatched her wrist with his hand, Elizabeth managed to twist her other hand free. Her hair had come undone and her green eyes glittered terror, her gaze darting in every direction for something or someone to rescue her. "I'm telling you again as you apparently have bad hearing. Do not touch me or I will not be held responsible for my actions."

The Fox leaped forwards before she could escape the premises and grabbed her around the waist. "You most certainly will be responsible for your actions, missy!" he snarled. "There ain't gonna be no more shenanigans from you, I tell you. I'm makin' it my personal business." He leaned in for a kiss, his grip tightening around her. She turned her head away from his hot, alcoholic breath and again kicked him in the shin. This time the force of her kick was not as forceful. She was too frightened and had lost most of her strength. Her limbs were shaking and her breath came out short and fast.

She felt the man's slobbery lips graze the side of her cheek. It was so disgusting she was sure she would faint from the horror of this entire episode.

Instead, a tall shadow was suddenly seen in the saloon's swinging doors. Every head pivoted towards it.

Including the Fox.

Elizabeth took the distraction to her advantage and scrambled backwards. She made it to an empty saloon table in the corner of the room, snatched something off the table, and then jumped on top of it.

In her hand was held an empty glass. The girl clutched it within her fingers, her eyes flashing. "Don't come near," she warned, her voice shaking.

The Fox, who had been in the process of chasing her, paused. He eyed her warily.

"Now, missy, I ain't never meant no harm. Doggone it, all I meant to do was to just have a little fun. And look at the way you're takin' it. Did you know that you are hurtin' my feelin's now, girl?"

"Your feelings? Ha! You don't even have feelings. You wicked dog! I ought to kill you for your actions to a lady."

The Fox's slimy smile disappeared for but a second before he quickly plastered it back on. "Missy, the more you fight and the more fiery you are, the more I admire you."

The girl huffed for air. "Well, when I attack your sorry, contemptible, dastardly excuse of a man, then you'll really admire me."

It seemed her words were enough for the Fox. He reached into his holster and slid out his handgun in fluid motion. "Missy, I'm warnin' you too. Get off that table or you'll be blown to pieces!"

Chapter Twelve

The girl did not even blink as the pistol was aimed at her. She didn't flinch but instead continued to stand there, proud and arrogant.

"Girl…" The Fox's voice trailed off.

Elizabeth raised one eyebrow. "Are you going to shoot me?" she questioned sweetly. "Well, by all means, please. Don't hesitate on my account. Pull that whatever-you-call-it and blow me to pieces. I would prefer to die a heroic death than allow you to touch me again…" *You wicked, vile, wretched man!*

The Fox's Adam's apple bobbed with uncertainty. Who was this wild, half-crazed, red-haired female? He had never before encountered any girl with such a contumelious attitude.

"Missy, you got a gun aimed at your heart. Ain't you afraid?"

She rolled her eyes heavenward. It appeared all the fear she'd owned disappeared. "Why, no. And why should I be?"

The men frowned, puzzled by her response. A low murmur rose behind him as all eyed the scene. Some shifted, edgy.

She continued primly. "I am not afraid because I have my husband who is standing right behind you all with the sheriff and his deputy. At least I believe they are the sheriff and his deputy because both are holding large metal weapons and both are wearing a gold star on his shirt. The sheriff is holding one very large contraption in particular."

The Fox appeared to disbelieve her. "Girl, do you think I'm

stupid?" he snorted. "That's a joke." However, his incredibility transformed to alarm as he heard the words behind him.

"H-he's got his famous sh-shotgun with h-him," the bartender stuttered with fear as he peeped over the edge of the counter from where he was hiding.

Elizabeth smile grew with smug confidence. "That's right," she replied, awarding the shaking, wiry man with a sweet smile. "I had nearly forgotten about that." She rested a slender finger upon her cherry lips, pretending to think. "Oh, and there is just one more surprise for you. I might warn you because you are right at the center of his aim."

The Fox's face became pale as milk. "Y-you're jokin'," he tried, as he turned his eyes side to side to see the reactions of those around him.

Elizabeth smirked, extremely pleased with herself. "All right. If you believe I'm jesting, why don't you ask the sheriff to shoot you right now? Once you are lying across the saloon in little pieces, will you then believe me?"

Fox was cornered. And he knew it.

He glanced over his shoulder at the big, burly man behind him. The sheriff tightened his lips and shifted his gun into a better position. "Yeah. Are you prepared for a night in the cell? It'll help sober you up a bit."

The Fox gulped. He smashed his fist against the wall before shoving his .45 caliber back into his gun belt. A stream of oaths spilled from his lips.

Elizabeth gasped. "I advise you watch your language, sir. Instead, perhaps it is wiser to turn around and march right on towards your ready-made waiting jail cell where a contemptable man like you belongs." Her expression transformed to raw fury. "Wait. Before you go…" The girl jumped off the table and marched up to him. She reached out and slapped his cheek so hard that her hand tingled as a result. Ignoring the pain, the girl put on her fiercest glare. "Don't *ever* try that again," she hissed. "For if you do, I am only giving you one warning: you will not be alive to see the dawning of another day."

90

The men in the room guffawed at her threat. "Missy, no offence intended, but ain't you a bit too young and innocent to kill someone? Or stupid?" The man who had voiced the question jostled his friend's shoulder with a chuckle. The majority of the men exchanged amused glances, wondering what she would reply.

She tilted her head, her curls bouncing to one side of her shoulder. "Who said I would be the murderer?" She smiled her sweetest smile, her voice dripping honey. "I will leave you all to consider my words and let them sink in to your thick skulls of obstinacy."

The Fox's eyes darkened. "I don't like females threatenin' me," he snarled.

Elizabeth turned her smile on him, cocking her head from side to side, satisfied with herself. That lasted about another second. Her smile vanished as his grimy hand grasped her arm once more. She bit his hand and heard him howl as he loosened his grip. She jerked away from him and out of arm's length. "Don't touch me again," she hissed. "And this is my last warning."

Her words were washed away as David tramped up to the man and grabbed his arm. Fox turned to face him. Before the wicked man could withdraw his gun from its holster, David punched him directly in the abdomen. Fox toppled over, holding his middle. The tall man stood over him, breathing slowly.

The room was thick with tension.

"If I ever see you or anyone else touch my wife again," he said to the moaning man, "I tell you that the result will not be pleasant. Do I make myself clear?" His eyes met each man in the room. At each man's nod, David glowered at him. "Now, you all get back to your useless time of drinking and gambling. And don't let me ever catch you fooling around with my wife again."

The sheriff nodded. "That goes for me too. Either behave yourselves or you'll be locked up in the clink for the night like Fox here with a nice bail to come up with in the morning."

The men seated men scrambled to their feet and over half of them left the saloon. The pianist began to play again while the rest of the men merely slouched back to their chairs and began dealing Blackjack and Poker again.

David shook his head, grabbed her arm, and whisked her out the saloon. Once back on the street, the tall man took her by both shoulders and looked hard in her eyes. "Beth, are you all right?" Not waiting for her to reply, he let into his long tirade.

"What in tarnation attracted you to go in there in the first place?" he demanded. "Are you that foolish you didn't realize what you were getting yourself into?"

The girl's chin quivered despite her strong resolve to secure her emotions. She blinked back tears. Without responding, she turned and slumped her way down the street. David gently caught her hand in his before she had the opportunity to leave and get into more mischief.

His tone softened. "Haven't you any idea of how concerned I am for your welfare? I should have never consented to you browsing the town on your own! I ought to have realized the dangers and your inexperience. I am your guardian and I have failed both you and my father." His eyes met hers urgently. "I nearly died when I discovered you were in there all alone, Beth."

She did not answer but instead a silent tear rolled down her cheek. Her green eyes were filled with such pain that David himself was at a loss for words.

"I'm sorry." The words were so soft that the tall man had to strain his ears to hear them.

"What was that?"

"I'm sorry. I didn't know what a saloon was like and I wanted to see..." Her voice trailed off. Another silent tear dripped down. "I ought to have at least asked your opinion. I just thought I could handle it on my own."

David exhaled in relief. "You are all right, though, aren't you?" he asked, concern etched in his voice.

She nodded quietly. But words escaped her. The entire ordeal had been both shocking and exhausting, David realized.

"It's okay," he said, clasping her hand in his. "You're safe now. I promise."

The tenderness in his words broke away the iron that had locked her heart for so many years. No longer could she hold back the tears. She turned and wept against his shoulder.

The tall man held her there silently, his arms enclosed around her, feeling her pain. Elizabeth cried against him, letting go of all the hate and fury towards her past. Towards the pain inflicted in her life.

When she was spent of tears, she lifted her head, meeting his gaze.

"You're the only person I can really trust," she murmured somewhat hesitantly. "You are the only person I could ever call my friend."

She tilted her head up and their eyes locked.

"I think what you're saying is that you trust me." David took her hand in his, his expression warm and caring. "I love you, little sister."

Tears welled up in her green eyes. "And I...love you too, big brother."

———

Two days later

David was bone-tired. He yawned for what was the umpteenth time. He shifted in the saddle, trying to get into a more comfortable position. Suddenly, however, everything happened in such fast forward that David lost control.

A large black streak of fur rushed out of the woods ahead of him and onto the trail. It arose upon its hind legs and roared in surprise and anger. David felt a choking sensation of fear transfix through him. A bear!

The intruder's eyes gleamed a moment until the creature suddenly turned one-hundred-and-eighty degree and dashed off back into the forest which he had just evacuated.

David's horse reared up and whinnied frantically, pawing the air. His nostrils flared, and his eyes were wild with unease. Grappling for control, the tall man could scarcely grasp the turn of events. He pulled on the reins, but his mount only reared higher before his hooves thudded to the ground. Although the bear had already gone, he continued whinnying and kicking. Braveheart had apparently gone too wild for any human management.

David released his grip upon the reins and reached for the mane instead. The stallion whinnied yet again and then reared up so high that the tall man slid from Braveheart's sleek back, his fingers slipping from the threads of horse hair. His body hit the hard packed earth with a solid thud before everything went black.

———

When Elizabeth had first seen that demented black bear come streaking out of the bushes in the distance, she had been amazed. Unable to move, think, or do anything. All she could do was simply stare, her heart in her throat. Upon seeing that bear take off back into the forest once more, her trembling body slowly began to relax. But then the big stallion had begun to rear, half-crazed from fear, and upon seeing David go whipping up and down in the air, Elizabeth had lost any sense of control. She'd screamed in panic.

Her mount, however, had responded immediately to the shout by turning sharply and galloping quickly back the way they had come. The girl bounced all over the saddle, trying desperately to stay on. By some unknown force, she had enough strength to apply pressure to the reins until Wildfire stopped, nostrils *whooshing* with obvious anxiety at the situation.

Dismounting quickly, the girl shakily led her horse back towards David who lay still upon the ground. Upon arrival, she quickly tied the reins securely around a tree branch and then turned to David. Her breath caught in her throat. He looked gray, undoubtedly from the fright he had just received. But he did not move at all when she knelt down beside him and shook him gently. "David, are you all right?" Fear flooded her soul when he did not respond.

As she struggled to think about what to do, she suddenly remembered how Noah Harrison had checked her mother's wrist pulse nigh on eight years ago. She copied his exact actions and to her utmost joy discovered the faint beat of a heart. Gratefulness surged through her. Tears streamed down her cheeks and she drew his hand into hers. Then sudden reality struck her as she thought about where they were. *I don't know anything about this wild wilderness but I can't sit here forever! I need to find help. Surely there is someone around this backcountry land.* Glancing at the setting sun, she knew enough that in a few hours it would already be dark.

The girl made a rash decision. With a start, she leaped to her feet. She breathed a wobbly sigh and slipped through the trees away for help of some sort.

God, my name is Elizabeth Davison. I am in a very wild and vast land called Canada. If You remember me, then I am sure that the description of my homely appearance will not matter. David says You know everything. I am not so sure about that, but I will take his word for it now. If You are up there, I plead of You to watch over David for me. I remain Yours truly, Elizabeth Hannah Davison.

And that was her last thought before leaving both David and the horses.

Chapter Thirteen

Elizabeth waded through the tall grass, her green eyes clouded with concern. The girl quickened her pace, pushing the grass aside while she ran. She needed help. Major help. But could she find any settlers? She fervently hoped so or else she was running aimlessly.

She lagged before she stopped, breathing heavily. She needed a rest. Spying a log, she walked over to it and sat down. She rested her head in her hands, still drawing deep gulps of air into her lungs until she felt revived. Drawing another deep breath, the girl stood up again. She was exceedingly anxious to continue her flight for help.

She poised, lifting her skirts gently, only to suddenly release the fabric with a jolt as one who had touched a hot stove. What was that?

A twig snapped in the woods. The trees began to whisper eerily which had a hypnotizing effect on her. The birds stopped singing. The grasses around her swayed in the breeze. The setting sun disappeared behind a cloud. Everything became silent.

And Elizabeth was terrified.

What was out there? A wolf, perhaps? A cougar? She had heard of all the hundreds of wild creatures that were lurking about the wild woods of Canada. Could that be what she was hearing? Fierce, undomesticated predators? Predators that longed to tear her body into shreds and eat her alive?

Fear urged her to turn and just run. The girl took heed and bolted.

While she ran, thoughts flitted through her mind in fast choppy, bizarre sentences.

I must not get killed by any wild creature lurking about in this wilderness. I have come this far; I must get to the end of our journey and reach the Promised Land. I must find the gold pot at the end of the rainbow like Mama told me about. Oh, how I want to see the entire rainbow. At her next thoughts, she felt as though she had just been doused in a bucket of water. *But perhaps it is not meant that I will ever be able to find the end of the rainbow. If there is a God then surely He is not hateful. He would not deny a lowly indentured servant girl to find her dream. Surely He has a heart. I know I am undeserving of His attention but David says God is love. Well, if He is, He'd better prove it to me! I don't take words as truth. I take actions.*

Just that quickly, her strenuous thoughts turned back to David. *But David. I must get help for David's sake.* Sudden waves of cold despondency crashed over her soul. *What am I even thinking?* she scolded herself mentally. *I am living a dream. David does not even respect and think of me a person with feelings! I am being ridiculous. I need to face the truth head on.*

He won't care.

There, I've said it so I might as well say the rest of the harsh, yet realistic truth. He can take care of himself. He always has; always will. Why have I forgotten that fact? Or did I only try to forget it? He does not need me at all and he doesn't want me with him, anyways! I might as well stop running and just allow myself to get killed. Someone else is just as likely to help David as I. Who cares about me? No one has and no one ever will!

Tears filled her eyes as she stumbled on a tree root and nearly fell. A tear trickled down her cheek as her sore foot throbbed from the pain. She endeavored to control her emotions but failed. Bursting into deep, anguished sobs, she shook her head in sorrow. Because she was crying, she couldn't cover distance as quickly as before. Then she just stopped. Sobbing uncontrollably, she sank down to the ground and covered her face with her slender hands. The minutes that followed turned into an hour. And that hour turned into three.

Still Elizabeth cried softly.

The pain that had lain forbidden inside of her heart was finally beginning to end. And as Elizabeth wept, half expecting to have an animal pounce upon her and devour her, nothing happened. Except tears. Tears that fell like raindrops before a rainbow would beam its promise into the still thundering sky.

It nagged her mind that she was allowing herself to let in self-pity to escape the true facts. And although she knew how puerile she was acting, the girl deliberately forced herself not to think about it.

She wanted love; she wanted to be understood and respected for being who she was. She wanted...oh, she didn't even know what she wanted anymore. Her life was one confusing mess all confined together. She wanted something that could calm the listlessness of her heart but knew that there wasn't anything that could ever help her.

Where was that rainbow she was searching for? Why did it not appear? She had searched so long and hard for it, but there was nothing that represented a promise. A promise for a future of happiness and contentedness. All she wanted was peace. Beautiful, tranquil peace. A peace that was nonexistence within her heart. She was empty, lonely and despondent inside.

Annette had said that particular peace only came from the rainbow. The rainbow of peace. The rainbow of true happiness. The rainbow that indicated the way to Jesus' promise.

Oh, *where* was a glimpse of that rainbow?! And *what* was the rainbow's promise her mother had mentioned? Would she have to search for that wonderful peace forever?

But then cold thoughts washed over the girl in bitter, dismal waves of scorn and disdain. Sneering. Deriding. Mocking waves of condescension and scoffing disparage.

There was no rainbow! It was a joke. A ridiculous, laughable joke. Anything her mother may have told her about seeing a glimpse of the rainbow was a joke. Her mother had been wrong.

All these years I have been in pursuit of capturing a glimpse of the rainbow. All these years I have searched and searched. Through every valley and every meadow I have quested; not leaving a rock unturned or a leaf unmoved. And now I finally come to realize that I have believed…a joke?

Disconsolate, the girl gazed upwards towards the dark heavens. *Why did you lie to me, Mama?*

No answer.

Why, why, why? *You could have spared me from believing something that is not real. You could have told me the truth. But you didn't.* Another loud rumble of thunder evoked the still humidity of the late day. *Oh, Mama, how I miss you and wish you were still here to explain things to me again! How could you have lied?!*

———

In another area not far away, a small two-room cabin stood. It was surrounded by trees and wilting flowers from the heat and lack of water. A few yards away from the cabin, a small run-down shed was stood. The horses twitched their ears as they munched on the contents of a full manger of dry grass-hay, every once in a while stamping their hooves and twitching their tails to rid themselves of horseflies and mosquitoes. Their eyes and ears turned to the cabin as loud voices from within reached the shed.

"Cade, I I think you're bein' ridiculous. Why can't we just turn ourselves in and get what we deserve? Shucks, all their goin' to do is lock us up in the clink for a few years. It says so on this here paper that if we turn ourselves in, we don't gotta be hung!"

A bellowing voice was heard. "It's a trick, you dummy! Can't you see that this is a trick to get us to come out so they can lock us up in jail for a few days and then give us a poor excuse of a trial before stretchin' our necks? C'mon, kid! You really that naive? And I'm not up to a "few years in jail" anyways."

The timid voice was heard again. "Well, how are we goin' to know for sure? You are really skeptical of everythin' anyhow. Maybe they really mean it. Besides, even if we do gotta get hung, maybe we deserve it." A sigh. "I am just tired of running all the time. I'm thinkin' seriously of just turning myself in…even if you don't."

"What?" Again the roaring voice was heard. "Am I hearin' right? You want to turn yourself in? You who has so much potential already at your age? Don't be stupid!" The voice lowered to utter disbelief. "Sometimes I just can't believe we're kin."

The boy swallowed. "But Ma wouldn't like how we live. She'd be disappointed with us; I know she would. And why are you so intent upon showin' the world that we are outlaws? I don't *want* to be an outlaw!" The words burst out before he could stop them. He stopped short, stunned at his own admission.

The young boy had hit a cord within Cade's soul. The older brother was enraged. "Shut your mouth, Calder!" he thundered. "*I* am in charge of us. *I* am in charge of this gang. You ain't nothin' except a puppet." It seemed Cade's nerves and anger suddenly exploded. He swallowed several times and then spoke, his voice barely controlled. "It would have been better if you ain't had never been born! You need to grow up and quit this stupid baby act. C'mon, become a man!"

Calder Addison swallowed hard. His older brother's voice sounded as hard as flint and his face was as hard as brass. "C-Cade," the boy began slowly, his insides tied in a thousand knots of uncertainty and fear. "I-I try to do my share. I try to be what you want me to be. But I"

"No buts!" Cade roared. "You think you do your share? All you ever do is hold that there gun in your soft baby fingers and tremble from head to foot while I do the shootin'. You don't do nothin' else. I gotta do all the work. I gotta be in charge of the hold-ups. All you do is stand there, holdin' that gun in your arms, doin' nothin' else.

You make us look like idiots, Calder! Why can't you just be like Pa? He ain't never was as squeamish as you!"

Calder shrank back from his brother's piercing eyes. He licked his dry lips.

"I-I guess I just don't got that feelin' for shootin' innocent folks. I mean, they didn't do us nothin' wrong and then we just shoot them after takin' their cattle. They ain't no criminals like us. They make their livin' the best they can."

A muscle in Cade's cheek bulged.

"I don't want to hear any more of such crazy talk. We are the Addison brothers. We have earned our name around these parts over the years and I aim to keep it! What would Cass and Cole think if they could see how you're actin' now? And Connor and Cody? Why, they would be mighty ashamed of the way you is actin'."

Calder felt his heart pounding. But he just couldn't help but riposte his brother once more. The words flooded his mind. "We earned our names doin' what, Cade? To earn a poster that says 'Wanted'? To earn ourselves the fact of always bein' hunted down like wild prey? To be treated like trash? To always have to run from civilization for fear someone might recognize us and get us strung up? Cass and Cole are wrong, too. Killin' and stealin' ain't the right way to make our livin'. There is another way; I know there is. As for Connor and Cody...well, what do they really know? They just do what Cass and Cole tell them to." Calder shook his head. "And I don't know what you think you've earned, but it's nothin' Ma would be proud of."

Cade gritted his teeth. Why was his little brother talking like this?

"Just as I suspected. You really are too dumb to realize what it is we're doin'. I'm earnin' us money so we can one day have our own stead elsewhere. Our own ranch and our own cattle. Don't you know that Cole and Cass are down South with Connor and Cody, each doin' their part of this so when they come back up here we can make our own ranch and all live together like Ma and Pa would've wanted us to live? It ain't wrong to be aimin' to get our own ranch and to all live together, is it? No, of course it ain't! Pa even told Cole, Cass, and me to look out for you. To make sure you got a good start in life. So what do you think your eldest brothers are doin' right now? Fulfillin' our promise to Pa...doin' this all for you and Casey, Connor and Cody." He shook his head. "But then again, you have always been stupid in understanding even the simplest things. Still tied to Ma's aprons string, eh? Well, life ain't all flowers and innocence. It's tough. We need to be strong in order to survive!"

"Rustlin', stealin', and killin' so as to better ourselves in our futures?" Calder wavered in an inner battle. He shook his head. "Don't seem right. It just don't seem somethin' that is right."

Cade snorted. "You always in what is right and wrong? C'mon, we do this for our livin'! Ma would understand."

Calder shook his head slowly. "I don't know, Cade. I just don't know anymore."

The elder outlaw spat upon the ground, his tone bitter. "You need to grow up, kid. Get a grip on life matters. Holdin' onto a stupid law to better your conscience is useless. Believe me. I tried that life. I near starved. People just don't seem to care either way. No, what we need to keep in mind is the fact that we are our own men. Nobody can ever be boss over me."

Cade's voice was proud and arrogant. Calder shrank back, not knowing how to answer. Not knowing how to voice his thoughts. He was afraid of his brother. Afraid of wrath. Of disappointment.

"Grow up, kid. Get a grip on yourself! Want to be a man? Then *be* one like Cole and Cass and me!"

The tantalizing words from his elder brother struck a cord within Calder. He nodded slowly; reluctantly. "Yes, Cade."

The outlaw smiled a cold smile. His eyes narrowed. He'd always triumphed and always would, too. Nobody could surpass him. Not ever. He was his own man. And that would never change, he was sure.

———

Calder felt miserable. Defeat settled upon him. How he had wanted to tell Cade he was tired of outlaw life.

But he hadn't because he'd been afraid of Cade's wrath.

He hung his head. Ma wouldn't be pleased. Ma would say that stealing and killing were unacceptable in the eyes of the Lord God.

But Cade said there wasn't any God. Cade had said that God was only make-believe.

Calder didn't believe him.

There *must* be a God. Ma had talked about Him when the brothers had been little. She had talked about it to her sons; to Cole, Cass, Cade, Connor, Cody, and himself. Their youngest brother, Casey, had been but a mere baby then. Although Calder had been young, he distinctly remembered that Ma had read from a holy Book called the Bible. She had talked about right and wrong and about choices in one's life.

Calder blew out his breath.

At fourteen years old, he was dead center of all his brothers. Above him, he had three older brothers. Cole was twenty three, Cass was twenty-one, and Cade was eighteen. Below him, there was Connor a solid year younger, Cody was almost twelve, and Casey, at nine years old, was the baby of the family.

But then they were no longer a family. They had slowly drifted apart over the past few years in both body and spirit although they claimed they were doing it all for the benefit of the four youngest boys.

Again a deep sigh escaped the boy.

Oh, how he wished Ma were still alive. If only that accident hadn't happened. The accident that he was blamed for. If only he could undo the past…if only he could see Ma one more time…tell her he was sorry for all the things he had committed to aggravate her.

But it wasn't any use. She was gone. Dead. In a cold, dark grave.

He almost wished they would get caught during their rustlings so he would be hanged and just escape this miserable life. The one thing that kept him going was his mother's voice as it echoed through his mind. *"Calder, life can be hard. Life can seem like it is going to destroy you. But never give up. Don't ever become bitter by it."*

The boy swallowed the lump in his throat, rapidly blinking away the few tears that welled in his eyes. It wouldn't do him any good to be seen crying at fourteen years old! Cade would josh him mercilessly about it until the day of his death.

Ma had talked about God and about His love for the world. About a Savior called Jesus Christ who had come down from heaven to save a dark world from an eternity of fire and brimstone. But one question remained. Where could he find this God?

Slouching his shoulders, Calder sighed. His job remained. A gunman. A job to assist his brothers in murder. In rustling. In stealing. In lying. In cheating.

And the worst thing that hit him was the fact that there wasn't any way out of it.

Chapter Fourteen

Every storm begins with one drop of rain. That first drop landed on Elizabeth's clasped hands.

The sky began to darken with intensity. One drop became two drops, which then turned into a light drizzle. The light drizzle became a downpour which transformed into a raging storm. The trees blustered and the grasses bowed to the wind that roared through them. A jagged streak of lightning lit up the dark sky while ominous thunder shook the earth.

Elizabeth didn't appear to notice. Although tears no longer ran down her face, her heart continued to cry.

She had lost all the faith in God her mother had begged her to never forsake. She had hardened her heart against Him. She was a fool…like every other person had been when they'd turned back from the pot of gold. She had ventured too far from the glorious rainbow's end. She was lost.

But deep within her soul, oh, how she wished she could be found!

If there even was a God, then she was asking Him from the bottom of her heart to help her. David said God cared about her. Elizabeth highly doubted that. All He really cared about was Himself and His favored people. She was nothing but a worm in His eyes. He was incontrovertibly just waiting to trample upon her very existence with the heel of His boot. *But what have I done to have angered Him so?* she wondered despondently.

Her heart hardened. Nothing. She'd done nothing at all wrong. Only this God seemed to think she had! And the long and painful way to end it was to simply allow David Harrison to pass away. Then Elizabeth would stand not a chance to survive this rough land. She would die a slow and antagonizing death of starvation. God would deliberately make her die a slow death. He wouldn't just end her life quickly, but He'd do it slowly…all because He *wanted* to hurt her.

Her stomach plummeted at the thought.

Why had she ever even attempted to listen to David's words? Perhaps God loved David because David was rich and good. But as for her…no, she was worthless. Completely worthless in His eyes. It didn't matter how hard she tried to please Him because He was determined to wish her life *adieu*.

But David said God loves you! her mind screamed at her reasoning. Then another voice spoke up.

It was a cold, hissing sound. Like a snake.

David lied to you. David hates you. God hates you. It is useless to even live anymore. Just kill yourself quickly now. Kill yourself to protect yourself from the slow and painful death God has planned for you to endure. After you die, everything will be so peaceful. No more tears. No more pain. Oh yes, everything will be perfect. Kill yourself now. The faster the better.

Elizabeth shuddered at the voice that hissed through her ears and mind. It sounded so vehement. So violent. So wicked.

The girl tightened her lips. She would not hearken unto its voice. The little snake would not sway her. Even though she knew she was being kept close tabs on by God's evil eye, she still wanted to live.

If I have to die a devastating death, I still don't want to miss out on my life. I have come so far. From England to Canada. The least I can do is try stay alive…until God decides that He just can't stand my miserable existence any longer and wishes me a sardonic goodbye forever.

David Harrison groaned as he regained consciousness. When he opened his eyes, raindrops pounded on his face.

He turned his head to the side to avoid the drops. Through the depressing downpour, he spied his stallion and Elizabeth's mare pressing close to the trees to gain the little coverage they offered.

Elizabeth.

Ignoring the dancing stars that blurred his vision for a moment, he jumped up, gritting his teeth in frustration as pain and darkness engulfed him. And he fell. Hitting the ground like a rock he lay there still, except for his slight breathing.

Raindrops splashed onto his still form, puddles began to grow around him while the rain soaked his clothes. The ground ran with an inch of water on it, and the horses dripped. Thunder boomed and lightning cracked periodically in the sky.

But David was oblivious to the storm raging about him. He was dreaming a wonderful dream that they were already at their new home. Tiny little shoots of green grass were beginning to show above the rich soil and the sun was peeking out from behind majestic golden-wreathed mountains. Distant ranges rose up high in beautiful blue peaks while the first ray of sunlight touched the corner of their beautiful log home. The fields glistened of freshly laid dew as the sun gently bathed them. Steam poured off the grass and rose up into the sky above like an offering to God.

Elizabeth stood by the cabin door, smiling. Those glorious tresses of thick reddish-auburn hair whispered their own song in the breeze. The wind teased her tendrils as they spiraled around in circles by the sides of her cheeks. Her green eyes sparkled in iridescent green. Her cheekbones were frosted with a becoming light of roseate, and her smile was wide with a fulfilled sense of contentedness. She was a vision of true happiness and cheerful gladness.

In his unconsciousness, David smiled. Perhaps he smiled at the irony of it because nothing was as he imagined…

———

Other than the slight drizzle of rain that continued to fall, it was obvious the predominant energy of the storm was spent. The ground was soft; puddles of water had formed over the squishy mud. Small rivulets flowed gently, converging into many streams over the ground.

In the darkening woods a tall wizened man stood, his gun dangling from his dark leathery hands. The austere figure stood still in the closing darkness.

His long, white beard reached the mid-section of his body, moving in rhythm with the surrounding trees. Long uneven hair bristled the back of his neck. He twitched uncomfortably. The clouds moved back and forth listlessly.

The old man merely stood and looked ahead of him; towards the mountains that rose up and reached the grey colored sky. But he wasn't gazing at the sun-setting mountain. He was watching the person he had cautiously followed.

The small figure huddled down against a large rock. He could see the dark shadow of thick hair and again wondered who it was. Curiosity overcame caution and he approached this intruder. He held his Winchester Model 1866 "Yellow Boy" in an easy but ready grip lest the person move and attempt an attack.

He gently poked the butt of his rifle at the arm. The person sat up, blinking in confusion. The man stared at her in surprise. She was a female! The question was, what was she doing here? He studied her, his eyes piercing.

She was not what one would call extremely petite, but she had a slightness in her build that made her look vulnerable. From the outline of her face, he saw high cheekbones and long, dark lashes. Waves of thick, red hair coiled over her shoulder. Her braid had come partially undone, he noted, and a few wavy strands slipped down. They wreathed the sides of her face as though to enhance the young beauty, all the while producing an impotent result. Her eyes were a vivacious green and freckles smattered her cheeks and nose. One quick glance towards her hands, and he saw that they also were dotted with flecks of freckles. Who was she? And what was she doing out here all by herself in this vast wilderness?

When her eyes phased upon his intimidating appearance, however, the confusion that he'd seen before, disappeared, registering into shock and then raw terror. She struggled to rise as though trying to escape his piercing eyes. He knew that he should reassure her yet he didn't know what to say. His words came out much different than intended.

"What are you doin' out here in the woods, girl?"

The young girl jumped as though he'd shouted a profanity. She stared up at him, unsure of what she ought to expect next. The old man glared down at her. She cringed.

"Cat got your tongue?" he asked, his frown furrowing deeper than before. Still the girl stared at him, almost frozen in time. A small ounce of pity coursed through him at her obvious terror. But then it was gone. Was it his fault she refused to speak? He was trying to help, wasn't he? She would die if she didn't find some sort of shelter soon. She needed a warm fire too. A body all alone with no means of defense out in the wilderness was just asking for a devastating end.

"I ain't out to pester you, girl. But I'd sure appreciate it if you'd set my mind at rest by tellin' me what you're doin' out here."

The girl continued to gape at him. He shifted one foot awkwardly, the first sign of any nervousness. *Nervousness?* The man shook his head. *No, I ain't nervous at all. I'm just feelin'...uncomfortable.*

"Girl, ain't you aware that winter is just around the corner?"

That seemed to open up her vocals.

"Sir, I..." She paused, obviously uncertain what to say next. She swallowed and forced herself to continue. "I am lost, I'm afraid."

"Lost?"

She nodded. "Yes, sir. I was trying to find help for my... husband...and I heard something crunching on the decayed leaves. I was so frightened that I turned and ran." A look of horror crossed her features as she suddenly thought about his mysterious appearance. She drew a deep breath. "Sir, was it *you* that was the 'something'?"

He nodded, no recognizable look of friendship upon his countenance.

The girl swallowed visibly. "Oh," she replied in a small voice.

She sounds like a mouse, he thought, disgust crossing his menacing face. The look obviously intimidated her even more. She cleared her throat, desperately trying to overcome her terror of the elderly man in front of her. "I am uncertain, sir, of who you are..."

Well, it appeared she would need to be uncertain longer because he wouldn't expose any of his life to her or anyone, undoubtedly ever. He just needed to set her back in the way she'd come.

"Ain't none of your business, girl, who I am or why I'm here. Now if you'd just explain to me why *you're* here and where *you're* from, I'll certainly try to send you back."

His words must have sounded harsh to her ears for she drew back farther against the rock the instant he'd spoken. Swallowing hard, she responded using the most dignity she could muster. "I was just wondering seeing how you just appeared so suddenly." She drew a breath. "I apologize if the question was discourteous but I assure you that was not my intention." Then she drew back her shoulders with a composed air. "However, sir, I see no reason to relay all of my information of my whereabouts to you if you refuse to tell me about yourself."

Her response angered him a little but at the same time he felt some sort of respect for this young girl in front of himself. She certainly had dignity. More then he'd have given credit for. He'd supposed her a dim-witted female. And she *was*. But it seemed she did have some brains left.

"I suppose I'm seein' your point." The old man shifted his foot and cleared his throat. Awkwardness settled between them. The girl looked down at her fingertips while he gazed off into the woods.

He wondered who she was and why she was here. If she wouldn't tell him about herself, however, where would that leave her?

She would die. Plain and simple. There wasn't any way to speak the words all gentle and sweet. He had to be blunt. He had to say the words without first building a soft pillow for her to fall upon when she heard the hard truth. The fact of life. He could see she was not used to a hard life of work. She spoke so high class and acted as though she were some high up princess that it made the old man nervous. Even just slightly.

He blew out his breath. Maybe some good would come out of this all. Or maybe something bad. The wizened man shook his head and tried to think of what to do next. He was in a fix, all right.

This land did not call for people of her superior class and high-faulting words of sophisticated sentence structures. This land was coarse. Rough. Violent. Oh, beautiful it was. So beautiful it near about blew a person's breath away. But behind all the spectacular beauty, there was something else that lurked within its shadows. Hatred. Killing. Outlaws. Death. A strength of brutality and ferocity that all strove to be the head chief and the dominate bully of this land.

The man had seen enough of it. He knew because he had seen it all. Had been *in* it all.

People came to this land for a new beginning. But all most of them got was a bad ending.

How the old man wanted to get these shallow-brained, air-headed, pompous inhabitants out of this land. This land needed hard workers. Workers who would strive to better it. And *not* some ignorant, prim-faced, strait-laced Victorian female who would not dare to lift a finger to help with anything and who would undoubtedly screech upon even seeing a tiny worm.

No doubt like the girl right in front of him. She thought herself a royal princess who expected to be waited upon hand and foot. What she did not realize was that *she* would be the one to wait upon hand and foot *for* this country! Not the other way around at all.

This nation needed men and women who would be willing to clear the land and live their lives here. To raise their children. To raise this land into a country of beautiful freedom.

But this little prim-faced, dramatic female was not one of those people. She most definitely did not belong here.

No siree.

Not at all.

———

Elizabeth couldn't have believed her eyes weren't playing tricks on her. If a band of outlaws had been standing right in front of her, she honestly couldn't have been more surprised.

She looked up at him, her eyes lighting with interest. Who was he? And why did he refuse to relay his name to her? He didn't look dangerous, she decided, scrutinizing him. His eyes were dark and they seemed to probe right into her very soul. His white hair looked almost ghostly in the moonlight and his clothes were like nothing she had ever seen. His gun was held in his left hand, its muzzle a scant few inches above the ground. He had the resigned look of one who knew that at his age life had stopped giving and only took away.

"I don't mean to sound hostile, girl. I just want to help or show you back the way you came." He spoke quite impatiently.

Elizabeth grimaced. Why did the man continue to persuade her to tell him where she lived? What was the reason? She decided not to relay any information to him about herself. She needed to be unabashed by both his looks and manner of speech. He was just waiting for her to let her guard down. But she wouldn't let it down!

He would be in for a long waiting.

She decided to be blunt. Perhaps that would help the situation.

"I refuse to disclose any of my whereabouts to the likes of you. For one thing, I don't know you. And quite frankly, sir, I dislike you."

The man just gaped at her.

It was terribly embarrassing being the object of such a stare but Elizabeth refused to acknowledge that her humiliation was nearly at the end of its rope. She got to her feet and looked directly in his eyes. Her back was ramrod straight, and her shoulders erect with pride, dignity, and perhaps even defiance.

This man was a barbarian. Probably a thief and a murderer and who knew what all else? He had possibly even been involved in major crimes! The thought made her blood freeze cold. Whatever was she doing?

She was playing with fire!

Chapter Fifteen

The world spun. Stars whirled around. Bright one, small ones, little ones and big ones. Some were silver and some were black. They flashed through his mind. In the midst of the stars, however, he suddenly remembered Elizabeth.

He painfully crawled towards a tree where he righted himself into a sitting position. Leaning heavily against the tree for support, he heaved his body upwards until he was standing. Everything became a blur and tiny stars whirled around again.

He struggled to remain conscious.

Resting his head against the trunk of the tree, he closed his eyes, desperately attempting to relieve the pain his side and head continued giving him. Gritting his teeth together, he forced himself to remain upright. Uttering a prayer for help and strength from the Lord Almighty, the tall man straightened slowly.

Elizabeth.

Panic surfaced in his chest as he envisioned her alone in the woods.

Oh, dear Lord. Protect her.

A feeling of momentary dizziness overcame him before he shifted his body's weight back up against the tree. He knew not how he was going to find her but he knew he was certainly going to try. Ignoring the throbbing ache that again threatened to cause him to collapse, he drew a deep breath.

The moon suddenly hid behind clouds. Immediately everything became dark. Elizabeth looked around herself, half expecting to see an animal lurking behind any tree. A slight breeze swayed some leaves and she jumped. But she didn't jump from fear. She jumped because it came as a dazzling shock.

David. What if he did need her after all? What if no one would come to help him?

An appalling chill swept through her heart as sudden terror flooded her mind with a profusion of dangers that may have occurred in her absence. She resisted the urge to slap her forehead in frustration at her selfish thoughts before. Was he waiting for her return? *I must go to him now. But now it is so dark, and if I must admit it, I am lost and afraid.*

Oh, how she needed to return to David. The main factor of the problem, however, was that she didn't have an inkling of how to retrace her steps back. The only help for this situation entailed the old man.

At first the idea made her stiffen like an affronted slap in the face. However, as her thoughts were brought back to David, she reconciled herself. If she really would have to rely on a complete stranger for help, she would do it.

Turning to the elderly man standing beside her, Elizabeth licked her dry lips. She needed to ask this question. Before she chickened out.

"Sir," she began hesitantly. "Sir, I really need your help." There, that certainly sounded respectful. "I…I…" Elizabeth stuttered. Drawing a nervous breath, she spoke yet again. "Sir, my husband is injured. He fell off his horse and is unconscious. I left him to try find some help, but now I am lost." She looked at the man intently. He simply stared at her. Disappointment whisked through her. She could discern by his look he was going to refuse.

Desperate for his help and forgetting that she had just decided she was not going to beseech him, she blurted out the words which were filled with desperation.

"I beg of you, sir! I really need your help." Her voice cracked. "Please, sir!"

It was either her tone of voice or the tears that welled up in her eyes, but he suddenly nodded decisively. "Now miss, please don't cry. I can't abide with females bawlin'. Calm yourself down."

She dashed away tears. "Oh sir, I thank you! You don't know how much this means to me. I'm so worried about him and I can't help but continue thinking that maybe a predator has already gotten him for dinner, and…" The girl blubbered the words.

He eyed her in loathing antipathy and merely grunted. "Are you ready?" he questioned gruffly. "Where were you when he got hurt?"

She started. "Y-yes sir," she replied shakily. "We were on the North trail to our new property."

"And just where might your new property be?" he queried, aggravation threaded in his tone.

The girl lowered her lashes. "That is just the problem, sir. I do not know exactly."

"Well now, ain't this great." His scowling expression appeared to contradict his statement.

The girl reddened. "It isn't as though I deliberately do not know," she retorted indignantly. "I just never thought to ask."

The elderly man shook his head at her with obvious scorn. "Ain't that a female for you," he muttered. Then, "How far do you think you folks was out from Dawson?"

Elizabeth lifted startled eyes to his piercing ones. "I estimate about an hour," she replied, puzzled at his question.

The man glanced heavenward before awarding her with a skeptical expression. "Thank you," he grunted. Then almost to himself, he added, "At least she ain't as dumb as I thought."

The girl apparently overheard him for she stiffened. Lemuel ignored her antagonized stance and instead gestured for her to follow him. Elizabeth followed hesitantly, almost warily.

They walked and they walked. Her already tired limbs grew more exhausted with each step, but she kept on stubbornly. She relied on him to know exactly where to go although a nagging feeling continued to prod her. She couldn't help but hope that they wouldn't get lost in this godforsaken forest! How did the elderly man know where to go anyways?

Elizabeth frowned suddenly. "I have a question I must ask of you." She paused. "How do you know where you are going?"

The outlaw did not turn around. "I got my ways. Best keep your addlepated little head out of it. And keep that mouth of yours shut."

She glared at his back. How dare he call her head addlepated? Infuriated, she retorted indignantly, "How do you know whether you are not addlepated yourself?"

"I thought I told you to keep quiet," he growled.

Elizabeth straightened resentfully once more. Opening her mouth, she was about to give him the biggest tongue lashing he had probably ever received before in his life. But he spoke once again.

"And if you don't abide by my rules, you can go find your own way back."

She slumped her shoulders dejectedly, knowing he was her only chance of ever finding her way out of this dark and confusing forest and back to David. She decided not to aggravate him any more than she had already.

"Yes, sir," she answered meekly.

He glanced over his shoulder at her. She did not see his quick, perceptive glance and missed his twitching grin.

She was one strange bird, all right.

––––––––

Casey Addison felt tears spring to his eyes. But how he ached for his mother! The mother he had never known. The mother they never talked about.

One bright early morning in late June, Maria Addison had set out with a tin pail to pick berries for a pie. As the story went, there had also been a mother bear and her cub foraging for berries at the berry patch. The woman had inadvertently walked along a clump of bushes with the bear on one side and the cub on the other. The baby had called for his mother and the mother, having just captured a glimpse of Maria, had been furious thinking the woman was harming her cub! She had rushed towards the invading human, ending her life with a roar.

Casey knew this because of his fourteen year old brother had secretly managed to tell him about the traumatizing death. Calder Addison had only been five years old at the time, but he had witnessed the entire scene, horror precipitating his body to become frozen. He hadn't been able to move and all he could do was watch with mounting trepidation when the bear had launched herself at his dear mother. The boy had watched his own mother die, not able to do anything to try save her. No doubt that vicious memory would never leave his mind. Calder's spirit had been broken that day for he had never been the same.

To further advocate Calder's anguish, his father and eldest brothers despised Calder because they claimed he could have at least tried to distract the bear. Of course that only drew the boy deeper within the shell he had created for himself.

Casey had only been just a baby at the time of the accident. He had not one recollection of his mother although Calder had secretly filled him in on a few small things about what his mother had looked like.

She had been a reddish-blonde haired woman with sparkling green eyes and a sweet character. She had brought a smile to everyone's lips from her sweet attitude. Her considerate words and compassionate attitude as she listened to tragic stories told all around her by people was touching.

After being informed of Maria Addison's lamentable death, many a tear had fallen. Beautiful though she had been, it had been her heart that had produced the tears. It had been her kindness and generosity; the understanding she had bestowed upon others. It had been her heart-loving soul and the genuine sincerity she expressed for someone in sickness or pain.

Casey had heard all that. But he longed to know more. More about her. Of course he kept his mouth shut as most boys do about sentimental issues. Never once did he complain about missing his mother. Never once did his older brothers hear a single word of anything on the subject. Not one of them assumed nor suspected Casey was hurting deep inside of his heart.

Oh, how the boy hated being an outlaw. He hated the 'on the trail' life. He wanted security. But there was none in the life of an outlaw.

Nothing at all.

Chapter Sixteen

David stumbled through the dense woods struggling to regain control of the situation and focus on Elizabeth's trail. He tripped over a log lying across the trail and nearly fell, only catching himself by grasping a branch and pulling himself upwards. Where could Elizabeth be?

The snapping of a branch in the woods brought David's attention away from her. He stopped immediately. Footsteps sounded nearby in the night, and the tall man wished for a gun or a knife, at the very least. He suddenly heard a familiar voice. His pulse ceased. His head swam in stars and his vision became blurred. Everything became amorphous.

Yet his hearing still functioned perfectly.

"Are you sure you know where you're going?"

"Girl, let me tell you this: when you keep askin' me that question, I lose my sense of direction. You need to keep quiet!"

"Yes, sir." There was a sigh in the voice. "I am desperately sorry, sir."

David clenched his teeth together. It was Elizabeth. With a man. He knew they were coming towards him and that they were soon going to pass him. It suddenly occurred to him that he could climb a tree and then jump unexpectedly down like a cat onto the outlaw's back. Even if he blacked out again, at least she would be free.

He closed his eyes for a moment to better control the agony that shot through his body. He grimaced. "Of all the times for her to be kidnapped," he muttered through clenched teeth. "Did it have to be just now?"

———

"Oh, that hurt terribly!" The shrill cry pierced the air.

Lemuel Ellis Keagan heaved a deep sigh. This girl was really getting on his nerves. "What happened now?" he asked, trying desperately to keep the lilt of annoyance out of his voice.

"I didn't see a tree and bumped into it. It hit my elbow and even my nose! The pain is immense." The voice had turned into what one could call a frustrating whine.

If she don't stop complainin' about herself, I'm gonna just drop her. She about drives a man near his end!

It wasn't only her incessant complaining about hurting herself that made him upset, but mostly her never ending questions. " 'Are you almost there'?" or " 'Are you sure you know where you're going'?"

Lemuel sighed once more. This girl was definitely addlebrained. Even though he'd never met her husband, he already felt sorry for the man. Imagine putting up with the likes of her! It most likely was an arranged marriage, though. It was absolutely preposterous that any man would want to marry her of his own free will!

"Are we nearly there, sir?"

The question again brought fresh frustration to course through him. He responded abruptly. "Girl, let me tell you once again: when you continue to keep askin' those questions, I lose my track of area. You must understand that this is very important. Whenever you're in the woods, you must always keep silent. That way you can hear things." His tone sharpened. "Would you like to be out in the woods yappin' loudly alike a pack of stray dogs, only to have been followed by a cougar or bear?" He turned to gain her reaction from his threat. A grin protruded at the corners of his lips as he evaluated her.

Her eyes were wide with fear, her lips were parted and she turned around in every direction as though there might be one there lurking within the shadows. Lemuel Ellis Keagan could not help but frighten her. Perhaps that would keep her stupid mouth shut.

"Oh, I am so sorry, sir!" she exclaimed, her face transforming into a sickly green color. "I was not aware of the consequences. I beg of you to forgive me for my ignorance." Tears welled up in piteous eyes. "Sir?"

The wizened man felt a twinge of regret. Had he really needed to frighten her this much? The poor thing was practically quivering with fear.

"It's fine," he growled. "Best it not happen again, though."

She nodded fearfully, easing in closer to him for protection. "I will try," she replied, green eyes as large as silver dollars.

"Try?" He scoffed. "Missy, livin' out here takes a lot more than just 'tryin'. You need to work to succeed. Work to survive! And what in thunder possessed you to come here anyways? Are you lookin' for an early grave?"

The girl did not have the ability to respond. She simply gaped at him.

———

Another explosion of anger plunged through him as he heard the exchange between Elizabeth and the outlaw. As the footsteps approached, David crouched, readying to spring. But suddenly the footsteps stopped, first the leading pair and then the second pair.

"Wait here, girl."

Elizabeth sucked in a breath. "What's wrong? Is something wrong?"

David didn't move. His breathing became shallow. The rogue must have suspected something. Glancing at their silhouettes in the darkness, he saw that the outlaw was nearly upon the tree. Elizabeth was only a few paces behind.

"Sir, what's wrong?" Her voice rose in apprehension. Raw panic. "Is something out there? Do you see a wolf? Or a bear?"

The old man didn't respond. Instead he gruffly ordered her to remain quiet and to 'stay put'. Then with apparent unease and foreboding, he slowly began to look around.

David felt tension fill him. This wasn't going the way he had anticipated it to. What would happen?

―――――

Lemuel glanced around, suspicion knawing him. *But if that fool girl don't stop that constant yappin', I ain't never gonna figure nothin' out!*

"Sir, is everything all right?"

"Be quiet," he snapped impatiently, although his words did not come out so harsh sounding this time. A small bit of remorse scampered through him for being so insensitive. Was it her fault for him not being familiar to female children? He decided he had been just a little too harsh with her.

But I ain't a thinkin' of tellin' her that, though, he thought, his lips pressed into a thin line.

―――――

Horror paralyzed him. He couldn't believe what he was seeing. The man was holding a gun, aiming it directly up at David.

The tall man fought back the swelling surf of wild alarm. *If my life ends now, God, all I ask is please protect Elizabeth.*

―――――

Lemuel knew not whether it be an animal or a human in that tree, but he was certain something was up there. *And whatever it may be, I ain't about to die in result of it escapin',* he thought bitterly as he cocked the rifle. His finger was upon the trigger, itching to squeeze it. Lemuel set his mouth in a firm line, slowly pulling the trigger and almost…

"What are you doing?" the voice shrieked. The sudden yell caused his aim to veer off center. Fortunately, Lemuel had enough sense to jerk his finger off of the trigger before it might blast off, endangering someone's life (probably himself) due to her stupidity. Grimacing, the elderly man sighed.

It was that fool girl again.

Ignoring her, Lemuel lifted the muzzle and again aimed his firearm at the dark form high up in the trees above.

"Why are you holding that gun? What is it? What do you see?"

The idiotic girl was messing everything up. If only she'd shut up! But of course she didn't.

Clenching his teeth together, Lemuel squeezed the trigger and fired. The deafening sound shook the ground. Everything became silent until a large tree branch splintered and cracked to the ground.

———

Elizabeth screamed when the gun fired. Having never heard a gun go off, the noise terrified her. She jumped backwards, fell over a tree root, and then lay sprawled on the ground. The girl struggled to stand but her legs were wax. Eventually, she managed to get to her feet, although she was swaying slightly.

The old man's back was towards her so she couldn't see his face. Suppressing exploding tears, she had the sudden intent to march right on over to him. She did not seem to notice that the man's rifle was trained directly at the figure lying on the forest floor beside the fallen tree branch.

Instead, she was furious.

How dare he ignore her question? He was going to 'help' her? Well, he was a liar. This man was leading her on a wild goose chase. What a fool she had been to have been completely oblivious to his nefarious intent!

Both infuriated with herself for falling for his words that he'd help her and outraged at him for being a phony, she didn't take heed to caution and vigilance. She was going to get answers from him once and for all!

———

Lemuel Ellis Keagan heard the young girl's footsteps, and he heaved a mental sigh.

Female's definitely addlebrained. He set his jaw firmly. *But that ain't no excuse for any of her absurd shenanigans. Don't she realize that this ain't no game we are playin' here?*

"Get back, girl!" the man whispered hoarsely. "Get back to where I told you to stay put." Lemuel didn't turn to see if she was obedient to his command, but instead kept his barrel pointed on the figure still lying there. It was a possibility that the spy was attempting to attack when Lemuel wasn't focusing.

He heard the purposeful steps falter for a moment. But a few moments later they began again, only more forcefully this time.

Irritation rippled through him. "Girl, I ain't tellin' you again: get back where I told you to stay!"

Again the footsteps ceased. But this time a question was voiced. "Why, sir?"

That fool, insolent girl! Didn't she realize that now was not the time to ask questions? *Probably not. Imbecilic female. Thickheaded chit.* He grimaced, seething inside.

"Just get back and keep yourself quiet." Instead of hearing retreating footsteps, however, she continued defiantly. He couldn't believe it. Did she want to get killed?

"No, sir!" the girl exclaimed, her voice filled with vehemence. "No sir, I won't. It is none of your business whether or not I stand here or where you demanded I remain. The only business you need to have is to simply bring me to David." Elizabeth's voice cracked. "Why aren't you bringing me to him? Are you really going to help me or not? And what are you looking at? A broken tree branch? It's dead. You killed it for no valid reason. Let's go."

"Girl," he murmured, trying to be patient. "Please, be quiet. You're gonna raise up enough noise in this woods to awaken the dead! I really am aimin' to bring you to your David. I don't lie often, and I certainly ain't lyin' now."

Her loud sniffles ceased for a moment before she spoke up. "I am not quite certain whether or not I should believe you."

Wretched ingénue.

He hadn't needed to reassure her, yet he had. And this was her response? *If I don't die ten years earlier than my appointed death, I may die on account of this foolish girl.* "Don't believe me then," Lemuel answered brusquely. "It's entirely up to you. But I know my conscience is right when I say I am tellin' the truth, little miss. I can promise you that on the best of my integrity."

Ha! Not that he had any integrity left, though. He'd used it all up in his past years. Now he was as rectitude as a drifter.

Lemuel Ellis Keagan expelled his breath through his nostrils. "Now be quiet." Just as he realized the figure was moving, he added sharply, "And no more talkin'!"

His warning must have been penetrated into her thick headed skull of obstinacy for her response was rather subdued. A quite different tune then a few minutes before, he thought dryly.

"Yes, sir," she managed.

He shook his head at her, his lips thinning considerably. "Hands up," his gruff voice rumbled.

After seeing Lemuel's stony features or perhaps the gun two hands were raised above the head. Lemuel continued barking questions. "Who are you and what is your business here? Why were you spyin' from the tree? Answer me real fast and real quick."

There was no answer. The tall man attempted to rise.

"Move one more time and I swear I'll shoot! I might warn you that I got a mighty itchy trigger-finger."

The figure stopped instantly, and Lemuel scrutinized him. The man was well-cut and tall. His angular jaw was clenched, and his cobalt blue eyes darkened with intensity. But he was calm. There wasn't any cursing or smart aleck comments. Never before had Lemuel seen any man so self-composed when facing a rifle barrel.

Shaking his head, the old man wondered if this stranger really was a spy.

———

Elizabeth scrutinized the tall stranger. She suddenly realized who was lying beside the tree because the more she looked, the more she realized he appeared somewhat familiar.

David! It had to be David. Emotion surfaced, and she hastily rubbed a tear gathering in the corner of her eye. What was there to cry about? David was safe. He was alive! Confusion overtook joyfulness. She frowned. *But...what is David doing here?*

Gasping as the scene finally registered in her mind, Elizabeth's brain seemed to kick in. The girl scrambled to her feet and ran towards the tall man, completely forgetting Lemuel's sharp words to remain where she was. And as she passed his burly form, she felt some sort of accomplishment fill her. Yes, she'd save her big brother-like figure somehow. And nothing and no one would ever stop her!

Chapter Seventeen

Lemuel couldn't believe what he was seeing. Was the idiotic girl really running towards the spy?

"Girl, stop!" he shouted. "I ain't a tellin' you again. Stop and come back before it's too late!"

Elizabeth jerked to a complete stop, and Lemuel took this as the first sign to common sense. "I ain't tellin' you again. Get back to where I told you to stay!"

Anger surged through her at his commanding tone. "No, I won't." She tossed her head defiantly. And then she turned back in an insubordinate flounce to the spy.

Oh, that stupid, addlebrained female! Did not she realize that the rogue could take her as a hostage? Fear gnawed at his insides. Whatever possessed her to suddenly start running towards him?

The devil himself, the old man thought gravely. *The filly is bewitched!* Ah, that probably explained her strange reactions and dramatic orientations. Bewitched girl or not, the man before him needed attention. Very special attention, indeed.

Particularly from Mr. Winchester.

———

David stared, his eyes widening with surprise as he watched the scene play out before him until she was suddenly standing before him, breathless yet beaming. Beaming? He shook his head. Silly girl. He had a hunch she was smug about having gotten the better of the outlaw. David, however, had more important things to smirk about besides having Elizabeth by his side again. *What if that outlaw attempts to shoot at me, but accidentally hits Beth?* Terror smote his heart.

He grabbed her arm shoving her behind him.

"W-what?" Elizabeth stuttered, stunned.

"Beth, be silent!" David whispered hoarsely.

———

"That's it!" Lemuel's gruff voice cut through the silence like knife through hot butter. "If you want to live, explain yourself and hand over that girl."

When the old man saw that the rogue made no move to hand that young girl over, he simply shifted his stance, a sure sign that he had spoken the truth. "I'm givin' you one last chance, boy," Lemuel spoke harshly. "Hand over that girl or else it'll be the curtains for you."

The tall man spoke at last. "Sir, I am not a spy." The old man was surprised that the 'spy' did not take the offense side. After all, he had a potential hostage. Instead, he chose to take the defensive. What manner of a man was this?

Either stupid or sly, Lemuel thought graveled. His laugh dripped sarcasm. "You say you ain't no spy?" He shook his head. "Don't you lie to me, you knave! I ain't standin' for no wretched police spy."

"Sir, I am not a spy!" The voice took on a desperate tone. "I journeyed from England to my new land here. I got injured when a bear came tearing out of the woods, startling my horse in the process."

Lemuel held his ground. "You can stop your story-tellin' now. Why would an injured traveler climb a tree like you did, and why didn't you tell us somethin' more about yourself as we approached?"

"You just don't understand the situation, sir!" the stranger protested in earnest.

"Ah, but I think I do. You intend to take that innocent girl as your hostage, eh?"

This time it was the tall man who looked stunned. "Hostage?" he repeated, his eyebrows quirked with surprise. "You think I'm keeping her hostage? No, you are entirely mistaken. I am not taking Beth as a hostage at all. Beth is my..." He hesitated, uncertain, before plunging on. "Beth is my...wife. We are on our way to the land I just bought. We come from England and are seeking a fresh beginning here."

Lemuel weighed the words of the man before him. Although his story resembled the girl's, there were a few doubts that plagued his mind. It still didn't explain why he was in the tree.

The dim-witted female now suddenly phrased a question out of the very blue. "May I ask what your name is? I don't intend to sound ill-mannered, but I loathe not knowing people's names. Regardless, I demand to be enlightened of your name. It produces a damper upon my spirits to always have to refer to you as *the old man*. I mean"

Her voice trailed off once David jabbed an elbow into her ribs. "Be quiet, Beth!" the tall man demanded, his expression stony with frustration.

Lemuel Ellis Keagan didn't think it would be of importance if he'd relay his name to them. She would indubitably blather persistently in an infuriating way that would ground upon his nerves. He best just say his name and get her quiet. *Just* his first name, however. He'd not get secretly hijacked into giving unnecessary information to the two, just in case the man was a spy.

"Name's Lemuel." The elderly man spoke abruptly. "And that's all you need to know."

"Oh, thank you so much for telling me your name," she gushed beguilingly. "It is a pleasure to make your acquaintance. This is David..." She hesitated and gulped. Were they not supposed to be married? "This is my...husband...David Harrison, and my name is Elizabeth." She smiled sweetly. "It makes life so much more pleasant when we can put a name to a face, don't you quite agree?"

Lemuel eyed her but did not respond. This girl had obviously lost some screws. She was as dumb as a turkey!

The tall man elbowed her again. She was extremely daft. "Hush, Beth!" he whispered hoarsely. "Stop talking. You're making things worse!"

The girl shut her mouth abruptly but not before pinning him with a hateful look.

———

Elizabeth couldn't believe what was happening. She gawked at the man called "Lemuel" before her as sudden anger exploded through her. *How dare he hold a gun on us and for no reason, too! I wish I could knock some sense into him.* She frowned slightly. *And why can't I? Nobody can stop me. I'll tell that delinquent exactly what I think of him and why he is a good-for-nothing outlaw.*

She glanced up at David. The tall man was gazing straight ahead, his eyes never once wavering from the rifle. He looked ready to face his death if he must.

But if it's up to me David won't have to die–at least not today, anyways.

She drew a deep breath, trying to think of an idea that would work. A plan formed. She grinned surreptitiously. First she would smack David. Next, she'd begin to scream and cry. And lastly, she would attack him. The girl smiled smugly. Soon this awful ordeal would be history. Perhaps David would be so impressed and grateful to her that he'd reconsider his decision and give her some of his money!

She quickly brought her thoughts out of the clouds and back down to firm ground. No matter how enticing those notions may be, she knew that she needed to focus on the present. Not on the future. After all, that came later.

I should begin my plot right now, she fumed. *I'll show that David Harrison I am good for something despite what he may think!*

131

"Stop that, you ugly oaf! You cruel, hateful man!" Elizabeth faked tears.

Both David and Lemuel jerked their eyes towards her, startled expressions settling over their features. Good. She was already making headway.

Elizabeth turned and stepped out from behind David. "Rogue, I hate you!" she shouted angrily. Then she hit him on the arm as hard as she could which unfortunately wasn't very hard.

"Beth, what's wrong?" David stared at her, astonishment evident upon his features at her sudden behavior.

"How could you do it?" Elizabeth burst into alleged tears. "You pretend you're such a good man, ha! But you kidnapped me."

The tall man's mouth dropped open in astonishment. Whatever the reason of her babbling story, she was going too far here. It was one thing to make up a story in private away from prying eyes, but to act one out in public for all to see…well, that was quite another. Especially in the presence of a gunslinger who seemed intent to shoot him.

"What?" David exploded. "Beth, what are you saying? I *kidnapped* you?"

Elizabeth had allowed the tears to slide down her cheeks in rivers attempting to look vulnerable and frightened, but now she lifted her chin indignantly. Her demeanor transformed into arrogance. "Yes, you are an atrocious man, and I'm not about to keep silent any longer either. Everyone needs to know the truth about you."

What on God's green earth was she doing? Trying to make him get shot by degrading him in front of this outlaw and his gun?

He snorted. "What truth?" Exhaling, he shook his head. "Beth, you know we are come from England and that we are seeking a fresh beginning here. What are you talking about now?"

Meanwhile, Elizabeth was trying to think of ways to respond. That exasperating David Harrison was fracturing her plan with his sharp, intuitive words. But she refused to let him better her again.

"You are lying," the girl retorted, her bright green eyes becoming bright orbs of fury. Then she remembered she was not supposed to be angry. She quickly transitioned to her lachrymose act again. "You stole me from my dear family in the dead of night, and I miss them all so dreadfully. I had a young sister who was only a few days old, but you snatched me away before I could even say goodbye to her! I desperately want to see them all again." She reproduced an emotional sniff, delicately dabbing at her eyes, imitating the dignified and distinguished ladies back in England at the teas David's mother, Victoria Harrison, had entertained. This, she decided absently, was the only time she'd ever imitated such a charade.

She looked at Lemuel carefully, seeing if she could define any sympathy in him. To her shock, all she found was an immensely amused man standing there, his lips twitching ever so slightly.

Elizabeth was so shocked her jaw nearly dropped to the ground.

————

Lemuel Ellis Keagan was amused. This girl's acting abilities were clearly remarkable.

He chuckled. She supposed he would believe her sudden display of emotion and this dramatic act? Of course not. He wasn't stupid like her.

Around them, Lemuel realized that dawn was unfolding into the new day. Clamping his jaw tightly, he inhaled. Was he to stand here forever?

It's time to get some questions answered. This young man in front of me first says that fool girl and him ain't no strangers, and then that girl insists that she don't even know the boy! There is some real funny monkey business goin' on here, that's for sure. And I think it's time for me to get to the bottom of this strange situation.

Lemuel shook his head. *Fool girl.* She was the initial troublemaker here. If not for her, this mess would have already been taken care of. What she needed was a sound spanking on her backside. And not just a wooden stick either, but a wooden board.

If she were his daughter, he would have proceeded spanking the girl years before. In fact, she would have never even become as she was now. *Lord, if You are there watchin' this, all I ask is to keep my actions guarded. 'Cause I'm mighty tempted to give that girl a wallop she'll never forget.*

But she wasn't his daughter. She was nothing to him but a girl that aggravated him like mosquitos in May. The man shook his head. *Blast it all, girl! Thanks to you, I gotta deal with this situation. I hope you'll be satisfied when I am forced to shoot this spy to save your hide.* If she wasn't, well, he might just turn her over his knee and give her something to cry about.

Enough had been spoken. It was time to take action.

Chapter Eighteen

"Reach for the sky, folks!" The voice echoed through the woods. Elizabeth and David jumped, startled at the loud voice that cut through the silence as a knife.

"Put those hands up!" Another voice rumbled. "We have you covered so don't you try nothin'. Obey our commands or else…" And he let his sentence trail off menacingly.

Swallowing visibly, Elizabeth turned and glanced at her 'husband'. David's face was drawn while hers was completely conspicuous. Where had those voices come from?

"Reach for the sky!" the first voice yelled again.

Clearly bewildered, Elizabeth looked up at David again. The tall man was staring ahead, his gaze not wavering one inch as his hands raised a little higher. Elizabeth followed his line of vision. And then she saw them. She gasped, horror flooding her soul.

Outlaws.

The uncultured men had their .45 calibers drawn. Their eyes glinted dangerously; almost devilishly. David and Lemuel exchanged glances before Lemuel slowly lowered his Winchester to his feet. Raising his hands, the old man 'reached for the sky'. Elizabeth, however, thought rebelliously, *Over my dead body! I shall never raise my hands, humbly submitting before these wretched, vile men.* Resentment assailed common sense. She refused to submit. She'd prefer to die first.

David frowned when he heard the M1873 cock. Weren't his

and Lemuel's hands up? So why…? He caught on when the bandit bellowed. "Get your hands up, girl, or you're dead. Mark my words. I ain't never said somethin' I didn't intend to execute."

The tall man's heart lurched as he turned to see Elizabeth standing there staring ahead insouciantly, her hands hanging at her sides. Anger surged through him at her stupidity. *Does she want to die?* Quick as a lightning flash, the tall man snatched Elizabeth's arms and lifted them up high.

"Wh-what?" the girl stuttered, clearly shocked. Just that quickly, though, her surprise transformed into outrage. "Let go of my hands," she demanded angrily, trying to wriggle out of his grasp. "Release them instantly!"

"Beth," David whispered as he struggled to keep her calm, "You have to understand that we are in grave danger. You must keep your hands raised."

"But I…" She was about to broach onto another subject about how she could effortlessly take care of herself, but David interrupted.

"Do as I say," he growled, a note of warning threading his tone.

The girl eventually nodded, sulking. "Fine, I will," she snapped. *I suppose for now, anyways.*

———

It was preposterous! He just couldn't understand it. Oh, how he wanted to kick himself for turning such a deaf ear to their approach.

The elderly man observed the girl's puzzled expression as she appraised David's apathetic features. Lemuel, however, saw a young man conveying a look of "I'll fight until the bitter end". The elderly man felt some sort of begrudging respect form towards the tall boy.

His eyes turned to the girl. What was she thinking? *She is one strange bird who has a lot more to learn.* His countenance darkened. *Only if she don't get killed first.*

"Turn yourself around, mister!"

At first Lemuel didn't know what they were talking about. After standing there a few seconds, he realized that they meant him. He cautiously turned, careful not to make any unexpected moves. When the old man saw the two outlaws, however, his apprehension fled instantly. He couldn't believe his eyes. He'd recognize them anywhere! The two men must have recognized him as well for one dropped his jaw and the other raised his eyebrows.

"Cade!" The name burst from Lemuel's lips. He was nearly unable to grasp that the man he had practically raised was no longer a child. He had grown up and was now probably wanted for multiple murders, rustling, and stealing. An outlaw that had a warrant out for his arrest and, more than ever before, whose name on posters across the North West Territories perhaps even in other areas.

Cade Addison.

The boy who had been an accomplice with Lemuel in rustling cattle for nearly ten years.

"Cade, is that really you?" Lemuel breathed. He realized that his words had come out slightly too high. He sounded almost as bad as that fool girl. The elderly man quickly amended his mistake and lowered his voice. "Cade Addison?"

The outlaw pinned his black eyes on the old man and gulped. "Keagan?"

———

Elizabeth stared in complete surprise, her plan forgotten. She couldn't believe it. Glancing up at David, she noticed his reaction was also puzzled. His eyes sought hers and she shrugged. The girl's imagination went wild. These outlaws were indubitably an accomplice with Lemuel. The old outlaw had no doubt deceived her into believing he was going to help her find David and had secretly signaled to his outlaw friends to meet him at this exact place.

But she had been too blind and ignorant to realize it.

They had designed this plot directly beneath her nose and she was livid with herself. How could she have had been so naive to have not realized that? And now because she had trusted the outlaw, she had also brought David into danger.

Tears pricked her eyes. What made it worse was that this was entirely her fault.

———

"I can't fathom you boys are really Cade and Calder. I had suspected you were both dead, but here you stand, alive and healthy."

"How is it that you're so certain of who we are?" Cade asked.

Lemuel snorted at the question. "Why?" he questioned. "I have known you nearly all your life. Don't think I don't recognize you now." The elderly outlaw shook his head. His mind went back into the past. He remembered the boys' father, Canute Addison who had been Lemuel's best friend.

"Don't you remember how after your father got put into jail, he managed to sneak a message out askin' me to take care of you boy? I did as he asked. After you'd gotten caught near the Klondike River, however, I lost any hope of ever gettin' you both back."

The young men both glanced at each other, and then the younger one spoke, although hesitantly. "I remember our last trip down to get those cattle. Me and Cade was so sure of ourselves; so certain that the rustlin' would go fine." His dark eyes met Lemuel's. "You warned us, though," he glanced at his older brother, "we wouldn't listen. You told us it weren't safe enough to go around the town of Champagne but we didn't believe you was right. And we left you all alone up at the Lake Laberge."

Cade's grim facial expression oozed irritation towards his younger brother. "Calder," he snapped. "Shut your mouth and keep your sights on those two back there."

The teenager quickly jerked his sagging Colt back into position.

Lemuel Ellis Keagan watched how Cade barked orders and how Calder hurried to do his injunction. He saw a glimpse of fear upon the boy's face and the hard look of flint upon the eldest outlaw's, but

He heaved a sigh. "I told you specifically to stay here with your hands raised. Why must you always disobey orders?"

The girl swallowed. "I don't know," she admitted. "I suppose I just wanted to do something to help." She hesitated. "I'm sorry."

David closed his eyes. This girl was crazy.

————

Lemuel lowered his hands and walked over to Cade, out of earshot of David and Elizabeth.

"So, everyone will break your trust?" He demanded an answer and not a short one, either.

Cold perspiration eased its way down Cade's back. "I had it once," Cade dared to venture, "a friend who turned out to be a liar." He stopped short and felt himself shrinking backwards as Lemuel's gray eyes pierced holes into his being. He drew a breath. He couldn't keep back the truth now; he had to recount the entire story. Maybe then he could live his life without that pricking conscience of his breathing down his neck.

"I became friends with a boy in Champagne a few weeks before we went down to rustle and I told him about myself. When I finally dared to speak of my rustlin' skills, he claimed to be interested in that sort. I opened right up to him and he soon knew everything about me...and *us*."

Cade glanced at Lemuel to see his reaction, but the old man's face was expressionless.

"Well, when I told him our plans after every time we had us this secret meetin', he seemed excited about it. I began to tell him our ever move, first hesitantly as it had always been pounded and drummed into our minds to keep our mouths shut about our rustlin'. Over time, I became more confident in my 'friend'."

He again glanced up at Lemuel, his expression portraying embarrassment. It was obvious that he now regretted what he'd done. But Lemuel Ellis Keagan did not say a word. He kept his mouth shut and let the outlaw speak.

"After it was decided that we'd rustle some cattle from the TT Ranch down in Champagne, the next time we hit town for supplies, I rushed over and told him everythin'." Cade shuffled his feet. He eyed his younger brother who was still aiming his gun at the two newcomers and then glanced back towards Lemuel. The young outlaw cleared his throat. The guilt had hung on his neck long enough. The time had come to relay the entire truth.

It was now or never.

"And so he promised he'd be there. I cautioned him to keep silent and not breathe a word to anyone. He laughed and told me to loosen up a bit and that there wasn't nothin' to worry about. I took his advice, tellin' myself that I was bein' extra nervous."

Cade lowered his head, hesitating.

"I was walkin' on pins and needles the entire day because I felt so guilty about breakin' our secret trust to someone out of our partnership. When we arrived at the town of Champagne, I decided that perhaps the better place to be would be down by Lake Laberge. You disagreed and argued that goin' around the other way would most likely take longer but that it was better than goin' down by Lake Laberge where the North West Mounted Police were stationed. But I was confident and insisted. You finally relented and said you'd meet us at the TT Ranch. I took Calder along. While we was walkin', a loud voice suddenly hollered for us to drop our gun belts and raise our hands. I knew we was done for. You had been right all along.

"Calder and I were both handcuffed and brought back to the police headquarters at gunpoint where we were sentenced to work three years at a mine near Pelly Crossing. The days were long, the food nearly inedible, and the work back-breakin'. Yet we had no other choice. I was expectin' me and Calder to both get strung up, but the sheriff said he was gonna give us another chance because we were so young."

Lemuel Ellis Keagan silently assessed the outlaw before him. Oh, how well he could see through Cade's rough exterior. Every action Cade made, Lemuel understood. Every word of bitterness Cade spoke, Lemuel perceived as unrestrained hurt and anger.

After all, he'd been the same way.

Chapter Nineteen

Casey Addison watched the pretty young girl open her mouth and then close it again. *Like a fish out of water,* the boy thought, strangling the chuckle that arose in his throat.

The tall fellow beside her seemed to be near shaking her. His blue eyes flickered exasperation. The girl looked as though she were trying to pacify him but was obviously not achieving much. She frowned as he spoke harshly before her face crumpled and she settled her slender hands over her face, bursting out into a great dramatic wail. The female shook her head when the man spoke to her, and Casey spied the tears spilling through her fingers and down her cheeks. Something triggered inside of him. He felt a dull, throbbing pain flood his heart.

Crying. She was crying. Her sobs had him rapidly blinking away his own tears.

He stiffened suddenly.

What would Cade and Calder say if they knew what he was thinking? No doubt they would mock and taunt him about it. Casey straightened his shoulders and held his shotgun tightly. Alert. Watching. Ready.

"Beth, stop crying this minute."

The girl lifted her tear-stained face at his stern command.

"Do you know why I am so angry with you?"

"Because I disobeyed you?" she sniffed.

He nodded. "When are you going to think before you give into your impulses? You could have been shot! Think! Is the word so foreign to you? It *is* in the English language, after all."

She swiped at her tears, brightening slightly. His tone was beginning to soften. "I know. I will try think more before I act."

"I think that may be the only sentence of percipience you've spoken all day." A small grin protruded from the corner of his mouth.

She braved a smile up at him. "I'm going to pretend you are my noble knight who saved me from a devastating end of a painful farewell to life. I am going to pretend that you are the knight on the white horse who went out of his way to save a lowly servant." She gestured to the three outlaws.

The corners of his mouth tipped up. "You have been reading too many of those dramatic romances of kings and knights and princesses, haven't you?"

"Not at all. But I have read a few of those types of books back in England that the late Mr. Harrison lent to me out of the goodness of his heart." Then with a wistful expression upon her face, she asked, "Don't you wish that could have happened to me? To have a knight come riding out on his white horse to save me from a dreadful circumstance only for us to fall desperately in love?"

David quirked a brow. "Well, you *have* had a knight that has come running to your rescue multiple times," he said wryly. "And that is me. But then I suppose I don't match up to your knights in your famous books, do I?" He smiled wanly.

The girl bit her lip. "Well, you make a good *impersonator* of what it might be like to be rescued by a knight upon a white horse," she announced. "But you are still just an impersonator so there goes my dream, sailing directly out the window."

The tall man contemplated her for a long moment. She squirmed under his steady appraisal. Finally he spoke.

"Impersonator?" He could not help but grin. "Beth, your fantasy stories are all unrealistic! Can't you see you are living in a dream world, trying to find happiness where there is none to find? And where are you going to find this 'knight'?

She stiffened at the sarcasm laced in his voice. "It is not a fantasy, David. It is my destiny. Beyond being rich, my second greatest dream is to fall into love with a royal knight."

He snorted. "Have fun searching for him. Because there isn't a person upon the entire earth that could ever meet all of your expectations. You require too much of him for him to even show his face!"

She narrowed her eyes at his frank words. Yet she counterattacked him. "You are wrong. I *know* you are wrong. There is a royal knight with sun-bleached hair and cobalt blue eyes waiting there upon his white steed."

The tall man gritted his teeth. "If you came out of your world of make-believe fantasies, you would actually be able to see that they are all mere stories. But then you know that, don't you?"

"No, I don't!" she denied it vehemently although a cold shower of fear surged through her. Could he be right? Was she really only fantasizing her future with a knight upon a royal white steed?

The tall man shook his head. "When you come out of your world of fantasy, you will see how ridiculous you sound. For now, as you are so inclined to remain where you are, let us focus upon the situation at hand. Let's go to those conversational outlaws and explain everything." He turned to glare at her. "And do not speak a single word because you might say things that would result in a blundering mistake...as you always seem to do."

She nodded glumly. "All right."

———

This was taking too long. Cade had other things planned.

Plans that most definitely did not include dealing with a screeching female.

"I changed my mind. Get on your way. I won't shoot you."

The tall man breathed a sigh of relief. "On your word?"

Cade snorted. "Just don't question it. Now get goin' afore I change my mind!"

Without responding, David ushered Elizabeth away from the three outlaws. Breathing a prayer to the Almighty, he thanked Him for everything. And especially for keeping Elizabeth safe this far.

Casey was stunned.

Was his older brother really letting the tall man and that beautiful fiery redheaded girl go away? The boy's heart constricted. He just couldn't let them disappear. He had to speak to that beautiful red headed angel. A sudden flood of sadness spilled over his soul. How could he, though? He was an outlaw however young he may be. He was a boy that would become just as his oldest brothers. Even if he didn't want to be an outlaw, he hadn't an alternative.

Casey Addison expelled another breath. But perhaps this red haired angel could help him. *I will follow them. That way I can see if she would maybe consider helpin' me escape this life.* The thought in his mind, the young boy climbed down from his lookout tree and followed the couple into the woods.

Upon seeing them stop to rest at a laughing, gurgling brook, he crept a few feet closer until he was just behind a tree. An idea struck him. To see everything more proficiently he could climb the tree. The branch moaned as he swung up onto it, but Casey twisted himself athletically until he managed to sit adeptly upon a branch.

"Are you all right?"

He leaned forwards to hear the beautiful red haired princess's response.

"Of course I am fine. Do you think I am a porcelain doll? I can subsist whatever you can." There was a note of pride threaded into her words. A silence. Then she continued, her voice filled with chagrin. "I must apologize for everything I have recently effectuated. I never intended to create such havoc, and for that I am truly sorry."

"Beth, don't say that," David protested gallantly. "It isn't your entire fault."

Elizabeth shook her head. "Yes, it is. If I hadn't been so naive to believe that man was leading me to you, we would have never even been in this mess."

"Don't be ridiculous," the tall man scoffed. "You only did what you thought would help the situation. It could have happened anywhere and at any time."

She bit her bottom lip, hanging her head like a withering flower. "I suppose so. It just makes me feel sheepish when I think back to how I acted."

David sighed. "I suppose I was so intent upon reaching our new land before the day's end that I neglected to think of unknown dangers, like the bear and outlaws. I think the Lord decided to teach me a lesson in that I need to be focused on Him in times at all times."

Elizabeth's expression became bitter. "Oh, sure. How sweet of Him," she rejoined sarcastically. "He nearly got us killed in his endeavoring to 'teach a lesson'. Is that really a loving God?" She spat out the words with resentment.

David's heart plummeted. Why did Elizabeth always appear so acrimonious when she spoke about God? What had occurred in her life to make her begrudge Him so?

"Beth, I think you have God all wrong." She sniffed disdainfully at that statement. David sighed, offering a prayer for the Lord to soften her heart. "You seem to presume that He is intent upon hurting you, but that is where you are mistaken. He loves you but hates your sin. When you do things that are wrong, you are hurting Him."

Elizabeth swiped at a tear angrily. "And when *He* does things wrong, He is hurting *me!*" she exclaimed spitefully. "How can you still love Him when He does such terrible things to you, too? He took your mother, your father, and your little sister away. Is that really a God of love?" Tears filled her eyes unbidden. "I used to trust in Him because I thought He loved me too. But then He took my father. I was aggrieved yet my own mother said that it was His..." She choked on a sob. "She said it was 'His will' that He took Papa. I could just accept that." She tried to swallow the growing lump within her throat. "Life went on for a few years...only without Papa. One day I suppose God's dislike for me must have grown into such hate that He decided to take Mama away as well. I didn't even acquire the opportunity to say farewell to her. I took her for granted, and it wasn't until she passed away before I finally began to realize how empty my life would be without her in it."

"I am sorry, Beth." David touched her elbow.

She jerked herself away from his slight touch. "I don't need your pity, David Harrison!" she altercated. "Pity doesn't do any good. Never has, never will."

The tall man was surprised at the vehemence in her tone. "I know pity does not help ease the pain, but empathy is a way how we can express comfort as we offer condolences for a loss in someone's life."

His words were as a bucket of cold water that had been dashed across her face. "Oh. I-I'm sorry," she stammered. "I didn't intend to sound so malignant."

David had never felt such compassion for her as he did that moment. She had suffered greatly in her life. He now realized why she deplored God. She believed He had intentionally calculated that taking away her parents would chastise her for wrongdoings.

Elizabeth was obviously muddled in her thinking of God.

"God may have taken your parents away, but that does not mean He loves you any more or any less. It was simply your parents' time to die. God does not do things to hurt His people; He does things to *better* them in both their lives and spiritual journey. He did it because He *loves* you!"

Elizabeth uttered a short, cynical laugh. "He didn't do it because

He wanted to hurt me but He did it because He loves me?" She shook her head. "I'm sorry, but I can't believe that. Why would a God who loves people 'allow' their loved ones to die? Why would He make some people poor and other rich? Why would He allow some folks to die while others get to live? Answer that, David. Why?"

The tall man thought a moment before speaking. "Those are questions I cannot answer, and we ought not to ever question God. He is holy and perfect. That should be enough for us to grasp. God does not make mistakes."

The girl blinked back salty tears. "You can believe in that kind of God if you want to, but leave me out of it. I don't want anything to do with a God who favors certain people over others and intentionally hurts some to teach them a lesson. I'd prefer to be discontent than sing His praises to the skies when He is anything *but* praiseworthy!"

David was shocked. "Don't talk that way about God. It is disrespectful."

She snorted in a very unladylike manner. "Well, He deserves it!" she replied indignantly. "Anyone who favors some people over others deserves to be bad mouthed."

The tall man couldn't believe what he was hearing. "Surely you do not mean what you are saying."

She tossed her head defiantly. "I most certainly do."

Lord God Almighty!

David softened his tone, sadness threaded through it. "No, Beth. It is *we* that are the ones unworthy. We sin; God never has nor ever will. We make mistakes, God does not. We are the ones unworthy to ever be saved by Him! But God's own Son died upon a cross and suffered unspeakable pain so that we might believe upon Him and go to heaven when we die."

Elizabeth gawked at him. Her mouth had dropped open in surprise at his heartfelt words. "I-I never thought about it that way," she managed. "I never realized..." Her voice trailed off at the sound of a branch breaking and a loud thud. Whirling around, she saw a small figure lying prostrate on the ground atop a fallen tree branch. With a startled scream Elizabeth jumped backwards. Taking Elizabeth's arm, the tall man pulled her to the safety of his side.

Elizabeth heaved a sigh of relief. She was grateful David was taking charge.

Chapter Twenty

Casey had leaned slightly too far forwards when he'd tried to see whether his red-haired angel had a dimple when she smiled. Leaning forwards eagerly, he suddenly heard the branch crack under his weight. Casey fell with the limb like a robin's egg. He landed on the ground with a *thud*.

The boy tried to breathe, but no air entered his lungs. He tried to talk, but no sound escaped his lips. The trees above him faded into a blur of mixed colors, and then everything went darker still. His lungs screamed for air. Terrified, the boy flailed his arms out one last time, certain he was dying. But then he felt hands lift him, and sudden air filled his lungs. He took in deep gulps until his lungs felt they would burst before opening his eyes to the sight of two unfocused beings. When his shrouded vision finally focused, Casey was both horrified and stunned to see the beautiful red-haired princess peering down at him with anxiety written all over her features. And then he heard her voice. Her breath even fanned across his cheek.

"Oh, David, will the poor boy be all right?"

He drew a breath. She was worried about him! The boy's heart swelled and he drank in her concern.

"Oh!" she gasped. "Such a hard fall for you. Are you all right?" He nodded, still unable to speak. Her expression cleared. "David, he's all right! He's alive!" Her last two words were high pitched with excitement.

Casey drew a sharp intake of breath. Her voice nearly deafened him. He supposed he wasn't used to such a mouse-high octave.

"Yes, Beth." This time a low voice interrupted his thoughts. "Of course he's all right. After all, he's breathing."

"Oh," she responded sounding quite surprised at that statement. "I suppose you're right."

As the heavenly red-haired angel helped him up into a comfortable sitting position, he felt a wave of dizziness fluctuate his head. He blinked, turning anxiously to see her. He needn't have worried. She was still right beside him, and it made his heart leap to see her green eyes betray such disturbed worry. "I was very frightened when I heard that tree branch fall. I was afraid that the outlaws had followed us." She searched his eyes. "But why were you up in the tree?"

Casey gulped.

"Do not be afraid," she said gently. Her soft, silvery tone of voice brought small shreds of nerves to tingle up his spine. "You can tell me what is wrong." She smiled reassuringly. "I am not about to eat you; you ought to at least know that!"

Casey suppressed a grin. He drew a deep breath. "Miss…" He hesitated. "Ma'am?" He didn't quite know how to address her. He nearly blurted out that she was beautiful but brought his teeth down on his tongue to better conceal from her his thoughts on the subject.

Her eyes lightened exceedingly. "Yes?" she questioned.

"Ma'am…" He licked his lips nervously. "I-I just came here because I wanted to to see…" He buried his face in his arm. "It's nothin'," he mumbled.

He couldn't see the beautiful lady's face now, but he could still hear her sweet voice speak. "What is nothing? What is wrong?" Then seeing his head dip slightly forwards, fear smote her heart. "David, he is dying!" she screeched.

Casey peeked under his arm in time to see the tall man frown and shake his head in amusement. "Dying? Do you not have the ability to see he is still recovering?"

"Oh." The girl bit her lip. "But what if he is dying in front of our eyes?"

"I sincerely doubt that even is a possibility." David's mellow tone soothed her ruffled feathers.

"All right, I take your word for it. But I am just filled with so much anxiety for him. Isn't he cute? Do you see that little dimple in his cheek? Oh, I have always loved children with dimples."

Casey was insulted. Cute and dimples? Why was she talking about him when he was sitting right beside her? "Miss, I am alive," he croaked. "And I ain't no baby."

The girl bustled all her devotion to the boy. She smoothed his brow. "Are you certain?" she fretted. "Do you have any internal injuries? Any cuts or bruises?"

The boy shook his head. "No, miss, but I am just feelin' a mite bit crowded. You are practically smotherin' me."

"Oh, I am most sorry," Elizabeth apologized, jumping backwards. "I was just so concerned for your wellbeing. Are you all right?"

He nodded, although mostly to himself. Yes, he would be all right. He had to be.

———

David raised a brow as he listened to Elizabeth babble about how the boy oughtn't be afraid of her.

"Please!"

She spoke so pleadingly that even David himself had to glance her way once more to see if she really did mean what she was saying.

"Please understand I am not going to turn you over to the…" She stopped mid-sentence when the boy's face turned ashen and he tried to scramble up. "Why, what is wrong? What is it?"

But the boy didn't respond. All he did was try get away from her. Elizabeth grasped his hand tightly but she was obviously no match for him. Even at his young age, David saw the boy had muscle. Muscle that the girl didn't have nor could she compete with. He broke free and turned, beginning to run into the darker part of the woods. In two quick strides, however, the tall man had captured the young boy with one jerk of the arm. The boy was hauled up into the air and then set down onto the ground none-to-ceremoniously beside the beautiful princess. David, still holding the boy's arm tightly in his grip, spoke brusquely.

"Why are you trying to run?" the tall man demanded. "What happened?"

The boy stuttered a response. "I…I just wanted to go, that's all," he replied sullenly.

"Then why not at least bid Beth farewell since you had obviously taken such measures to speak with her?" David motioned to the red-haired princess.

Casey stared up into the tall man's piercing blue eyes, his heart thudding with fear..

"Are you even listening?" David sounded angry. Casey was a little frightened but then the princess spoke. Casey lost his breath, forgetting to breathe.

"David!" She sounded upset. "How could you even speak so harshly to that poor child? Why you ought to be able to see that he is but a boy!"

David gritted his teeth. "I'm only asking him a few questions," he protested.

Elizabeth shook her head. "No," she disagreed. "You are speaking harshly. Be kind. After all, you can no doubt see that he is a little boy. Don't frighten him."

Casey was slightly offended. He was not a little boy! Why did she continue to think he was? Would he need to get a hammer and pound it into her brain? "I ain't little. I am almost ten years old."

Both David and Elizabeth stared at the boy. "You're…*ten?*" Elizabeth squeaked.

The boy shook his head ruefully. "No, I ain't ten yet, but I can haul wood and…"

The tall man interrupted. "Ah, yes. I'm sure you can do lots of things. But back to the matter at hand. *Why* are you all alone in the woods? *Where* do you come from?"

Elizabeth intervened. "Can't you at least ask him civil questions?" Turning to the young boy, she asked sweetly, "What is your name?"

Casey turned eager eyes to his red-haired angel. He liked her better than the man the girl had called David. She was nicer. Much nicer.

"Casey," he said.

Elizabeth smiled at him. "Casey," she mused. "What is your last name?"

"I am Casey Canute Addison," he proclaimed proudly.

David's head swiveled around. Where had he heard that name before? *Addison?* He shook the thought out of his mind. A mere coincidence to be sure.

The boy turned a quizzical look towards his princess. "Miss, what is your name? Is it Beth?"

The lady's smile turned into shock. "Oh, heavens no!" She laughed aloud. "That is what David calls me although my full name is Elizabeth."

It was as though his heart had stopped. His expression showed the thrill he felt. "Elizabeth," he breathed.

The red-haired angel smiled at him. "Yes," she replied. "Yes, that's it. Elizabeth Dav…" David shot her a glare. She quickly amended her sentence. "I-I mean, Elizabeth Harrison."

"That's a right pretty name, miss," he said.

She smiled and tossed her red mane of hair. "Thank you. I think it is as well."

He eyed her with adoration.

"Is your mother still alive, Casey?"

The boy started and looked away. Her question pricked his soul. "Naw. She died."

The girl's blanched. "Oh, I am so sorry."

Casey shrugged, trying not to feel the tears prick his eyes. "It's all right; what is there to feel sorry about? You didn't kill her."

"You must miss her terribly." Elizabeth sighed. "I lost my mother a few years back as well, and I miss her almost more than life itself. Do you miss your mother?

David frowned. Was the girl daft? Of *course* the boy would miss his mother!

Casey swallowed. "Yeah, I miss her." The boy swallowed. "I miss Ma because everything changed after she died. Her death made us all different. I miss Ma because she was the only one who really loved me. She made me happy inside. Yeah, I miss Ma…almost more than anythin'." A change passed over the boy's features. He licked his dry lips. "Ma'am, I could probably do lots of stuff for you if…" He hedged. "If…"

Elizabeth looked at him intently. "If what?"

"If…" Casey didn't dare say anything else.

"I'm givin' you your last chance to give Alert back!" The voice interrupted the quiet solitude. The voice was rough. Gruff and hateful.

Strangely familiar.

Elizabeth shivered. Who was that?

David jerked his head around. *Dear Lord. Not again!*

Casey swallowed visibly. He knew that voice. He knew it as well as his own. Perhaps even better.

The voice continued. "Hand over Alert or you will both die. Anyone who tries to kidnap Alert will suffer the consequences!"

Casey sprang up onto his feet, looking deathly afraid. Seeing that, Elizabeth motioned for him to come closer to her. He did as she enjoined, and she held his hand protectively.

"You are back." David spoke calmly.

One of the outlaws came out of the bushes a gun aimed directly at the tall man's heart and sniggered openly. "Yeah, we're back," he sneered. "We're most certainly back. You have your hands on Alert. Do you think that we'd let that go unattended?"

Elizabeth frowned slightly. Who was 'Alert'? She opened her mouth to ask, but a side movement caused her to turn her head. It was obvious from David's firm glare that she not say anything. She acquiesced.

"Instead of ranting and raving at us, would you mind to explain who 'Alert' is?" This was spoken by David.

The girl opened her big mouth. "Why, you rude, inconsiderate brutes. How dare you accuse us in such belligerent tones? And if you a referring to Casey, then you ought to be horsewhipped! What is he to you anyways?"

The outlaw turned cold eyes on her. "Calder," he bellowed. "Get out here now."

The bushes crackled for one moment and Calder suddenly appeared. "Yeah, Cade?" the young outlaw asked.

"Get Alert away from her. Now. I got the man covered."

Calder bit his lip. He glanced at Elizabeth and then at Cade, a battle warring inside his heart. He swallowed.

"Calder," Cade barked. "You deaf or somethin'? Do as I say now!"

The boy tried to hide his downcast feelings from his brothers. He felt miserable inside. Miserable and empty. How he hated always having to capitulate to Cade. Yet he couldn't help but obey every word the eldest brother spoke. Cade had a way about him that always took down Calder's defenses or arguments.

Slowly the boy lowered his gun and slouched towards the girl. Calder didn't look into her eyes. His embarrassed gaze focused on Casey instead.

Elizabeth stiffened. She drew Casey back towards her. She would not give up that poor boy without a fight.

Her eyes flashed. Calder reached out his hand to take Casey away from her but she smacked it away. The boy started in surprise.

Elizabeth was fuming.

Her green eyes darkened until they became a smoldering black. "You will *not* take this boy away...you wretched, debauched, depraved outlaw!" She spoke low. Her voice sounded controlled although a small ounce of anger caused it to tremor. "I will not give him up without a fight."

Calder gawked at her. "He's my...my brother!"

Cade intervened. He aimed to fetch his little brother and get on his way to the North West Territories, not stay here and argue with a birdbrained female.

"Ignore the wench, Calder. Just take the boy."

———

David was fuming.

He held back from throttling Cade and struggled to control his temper. After all, what good would it do if he got shot attempting to restore Elizabeth's dignity? He remained where he was.

Elizabeth, however, wasn't about to let that go off so easily. Bright color flooded her cheeks. "You have no right to call me that!" she exclaimed angrily. "I am a lady; you ought to be ashamed of yourselves."

Calder jabbed a finger in his elder brother's direction. "Weren't me, miss."

"I know that. But your older brother is a rotten snake!" She glared at *him*.

Cade didn't appear to be affected by her fury. "I ain't sayin' it again, Calder. Get the boy." He paused. "And Alert, get over here right now if you know what's good for you."

Elizabeth quickly looked down at the child. The boy was staring at the outlaw with a frightened expression. Her arm encircled his. "Don't worry, Casey," she spoke softly. "You are going to be safe. Just stay with me; I will protect you."

Cade snorted, apparently over-hearing her words. "*You*...protect him?" He laughed sarcastically. "That sounds ironic. You can't hardly protect yourself!"

David couldn't hold back his anger. "Mind how you speak to her," he said tersely.

Cade turned and stared at the tall man. "Wanted to say somethin'?" he mocked. "Well, say it."

David drew a ragged breath, trying to steady himself. "I am trying to control my frustration towards you but am finding it increasingly difficult with each passing moment."

The outlaw laughed in David's face. "You're angry at *me*?"

David looked into the outlaw's face, and his eyes saddened. "You will reap what you sow."

Cade's smile melted away. "Look," he said, trying to make some peace. "Just hand over the boy and you can all go. That's my brother. I won't let you to take him. And that little red-head of yours best behave herself or she'll find herself gettin' a wallop on her backside."

Elizabeth gasped. "How dare you?" she cried. "You rude man; you ought to have your mouth washed out with soap!"

The outlaw's smile reappeared. But it wasn't a sincere smile. "Rude? In any case, it is the opposite. You should get your manners in place to *me*." He shook his head. "I want you to hand the kid over to Calder nicely and I swear I'll let you go."

"No, never."

Cade's smile was that of a snake's. "Then bid each other farewell. The curtains are closin' for you."

"You don't mean..." Elizabeth struggled to control herself. "You aren't really going to *kill* us, are you?"

"Yes, we are," Cade answered smoothly. "Unless you hand over that boy real fast, I may change my mind and let you live. But if you don't..." the man's voice trailed off ominously, "well, I'm afraid I'm gonna have to fulfill my ultimatum, ain't I?"

Chapter Twenty One

*F*ool *female.* Oh, if only she wasn't so stubborn. If only she would tell the boy to return to Cade. *Is she tryin' to aggravate that man deliberately? Well, if she is, she won't get very far. Cade Addison ain't the type of man to take backtalk from a silly girl.*

Drawing a breath, Lemuel pushed through the bushes.

Casey leapt from Elizabeth's arms. He ran towards the older man, certain that Lemuel Ellis Keagan would help the situation.

At that moment, though, big brother Cade lunged, captured the boy into his near impregnable grip, and then swung the lad over his shoulder. Despite how much Casey kicked and fought, he was helpless against his eldest brother's strength.

"Let me go now!" the boy shouted while he fruitlessly tried to squirm his way out of Cade's muscled grip.

"Forget it, Case." The man's tone hinted at anger. "You've had enough fun for today."

———

Hot tears welled up in his eyes. *It just ain't fair,* he thought bitterly. *It ain't fair why I am always treated like a little boy.* Casey wished for the beautiful red-haired angel's soft smile and sweet voice, but that was only a dream. Deep down within his lonely heart, a small voice told him it would never happen.

As Cade dragged him back towards the woods, a lone tear

trickled down his cheek. He hastily swiped it away in fear that Cade might see.

"I demand you let him go!"

The boy swung his head around to see his beautiful red headed angel standing with her fists clenched.

"What was that you said?" Cade stopped midstride and met her hostile gaze calmly.

"I said that I demand you let Casey go." Her voice shook slightly. That proud, arrogant man suddenly looked so malicious. She drew a breath to better steady her nerves. "He's but a boy after all, so please just let him go." Gripping her white fingers so tightly that they hurt, she blinked, swallowing hard to suppress the sobs that threatened to overcome her brave facade.

David, she saw, was shaking his head. She met his cobalt blue eyes pleading with her to be silent. But she couldn't. Not ever. She was going to save the little boy's life and future. She was going to protect him.

Casey Addison had stolen her heart. She felt as protective as a mother hen.

———

Beth!" David cried as Elizabeth suddenly began to run directly towards the Cade and Casey. "Come back here now. Do you hear me? Come back before you get yourself killed!" He almost took a step in her direction but caught himself just in time as his eyes turned to the gun in Cade's hands.

Of course the girl paid no heed to his desperate plea. She was going to show him that she would win this war. But David knew she would lose. This crusade would only end in disaster if she didn't listen to him.

Even though Cade Addison didn't utter a word, he still was in command, David saw grimly. The outlaw reached around a struggling Casey and swiftly drew his six shooter. In one quick, fluid motion, he had everything in position.

Seeing the grubby finger reach for the trigger, David threw all caution to the wind and rushed forwards, determined to save Elizabeth from certain death.

Seeing a quick movement to his left, Cade jerked his revolver, whirling laterally, while he squeezed the trigger in the same motion.

David gasped as the searing pain shot through him. He collapsed, groaning as his body hit the ground. The movement jarred his shoulder, and he swam in a sea of diamonds. Just before unconsciousness, he heard Elizabeth's piercing scream. And then everything became black.

———

"David, oh David!" she screamed as she watched him fall. The girl turned, leaving Cade and a smoking gun behind her. She stumbled her way towards the now fallen man, her vision marred by tears. She barely reached him as her knees buckled, and she sank down to the ground, hands shaking. She touched his fingers with one of her clammy hands. Her tears renewed as his hand squeezed hers gently as though to reassure her that he was going to be fine.

Yet he wasn't.

She knew that she had done this to him. She hadn't outright grabbed the gun and fired a bullet into him. No, she had done it a different way by disobeying his orders. Deep in her heart, she had known he was right and that she wouldn't prevail over the outlaws, but she hadn't wanted to listen. She'd wanted to prove that she could succeed. Now she knew where pride and stubbornness got one. It either affected others around you or it got yourself chastised and injured. As she sobbed tears of sorrow, she knew it was too late. She was repentant now, but David was still dying.

"Please forgive me, David!" she implored, tears streaming down her cheeks. "For taking your life from you, I should be the one lying here." Her voice rose and ended into an ear-piercing screech. "Did you hear that? I killed you. You are dead because of me. I am a murderer!" A tear splashed upon his hand. She did not appear to notice. "I could pray to God and beg Him to heal you, but...He wouldn't answer anyways. What did I do wrong to have angered Him so? Am I really so wicked that He can't even save you in response to my pleas?"

"Miss?"

Elizabeth turned to her right and saw young Casey standing beside her. "Casey!" she exclaimed, swiping at rivers flowing down her cheeks. However, it really did no good for instead of rubbing them away, the tears only smudged lines upon her skin.

The nine year old didn't respond. He gazed at her in silent adoration. She was such a beautiful red-haired angel. Her luminous green eyes glistened from tears, and her lips were the color of cherries. Her pale skin was dusted in freckles that appeared upon her hands, cheeks and nose.

Behind her a deep voice spoke. "I need to tend to the man, girl. Best you move."

She looked up into Lemuel Ellis Keagan's eyes and bit back sobs that arose within her throat. After rising, she turned around, shocked to see both Cade and Calder directly in front of her. Her surprise at seeing the two of them faded, anger replacing it. Glaring up at Cade, she spoke harshly, her little teeth clenched in fury. "If you hadn't held us up, this wouldn't have occurred."

Much to her astonishment, Cade Addison did not respond and instead coolly met her gaze as though he saw this every day, although she wouldn't doubt he did. She opened her mouth to say something more, but at that moment the elderly man interrupted their conversation.

"Quit your squabblin'!" he thundered, kneeling down at David's side and unbuttoning his shirt to expose the bullet wound. "Back out of the way all of you." The wizened man spoke harshly. "I can't see the wound because you are makin' shadows on his shoulder."

Cade and Calder moved out of the way. Elizabeth stood there dumbly. Lemuel frowned in irritation. "Are you deaf, girl?" he shouted, clearly agitated.

She jumped. "No, sir, I am not. But I most certainly shall be if you continue to speak that way to me in such a tone."

"Well, that is most certainly a relief." His patience was clearly running thin. "So now that it's all cleared up that you ain't got no hearin' problem, would you mind to move?"

She looked startled. "Of course. I am sorry," she murmured, looking embarrassed.

Lemuel turned to Calder. "Help me by holdin' up his arm."

The outlaw dutifully came and knelt down, lifting the arm a bit more away from the tall man's body. "Bullet's lodged pretty deep," he muttered to himself.

Her green eyes pooled as she glanced once more at David, and her heart swelled with an ocean of tears. She blinked rapidly before speaking. "I would like to hold a truce between us. Why can't we discard of our opinions and disagreements for now?"

They considered her words. After what seemed an eternity, Cade spoke. "I suppose there ain't any harm in unitin' in this. Although it ain't generally our way, in this case I suppose we can be lenient. We will hold a truce."

The girl breathed a sigh of relief even though her eyes still spit sparks of fire towards him. "Thank you," she replied almost sarcastically. "It is greatly appreciated. I most certainly am pledged and beholden to you for such a generous offer."

Cade's lips twitched. "But if you don't behave yourself, little lady, the truce ends immediately. Do not forget that we are still enemies."

Elizabeth lifted her chin. "I have no intention of forgetting that, I assure you."

"Oh, I'm sure you won't. Especially not with my six shooter on hand."

The red head narrowed her eyes. "Your innuendo has been

apprehended. There will be no need of violence." *At least not at present,* she added mentally.

"I'm glad that is straightened out," Cade remarked coolly. "Because I'm sure you wouldn't like to be shot down along with your man."

Elizabeth struggled to control her rising fury. "You wicked man," she hissed. "You ought to be locked behind bars for life!"

The outlaw's tone sharpened. "Miss, I wouldn't say that if I was you. It ain't nice and it ain't smart. Your smart-aleck tongue seems to be your main downfall. It ain't gonna be as surprising as a blizzard in July if I do end up shootin' you after all. Behave yourself and you may have the opportunity to live until comin' daylight."

"Are you insinuating that I will be murdered if I do not behave myself?" Elizabeth shrieked indignantly. "Because I have no intention of developing 'submission' to the likes of a dirty, low-down ogre who calls himself a man!"

Cade's jaw locked. Enough was enough. She had overstepped his tolerance line. He took a step forwards and grasped her arm. "Now look here, missy," he intimidated, towering over her. "I ain't standin' for any back-talk. You shut your mouth right now if you know what's good for you."

Elizabeth attempted to jerk out of his grasp. He held fast and locked gazes. "Do you understand what I am suggestin'? Your life could end sooner than you are expectin'."

Sudden fear washed over the girl. Here was an outlaw, and she was actually retorting with words that could end her life?

Cade's jaw tightened...as did his grip. "I asked you a question, girl. Now give me an answer."

She swallowed hard, hating herself for having to admit that she was frightened of the rough and barbaric man. "Yes." She all but bit out the word.

Cade nodded, apparently satisfied by her one-worded sullen admission. "That's better." He then released her arm also inadvertently giving her a shove.

Elizabeth stumbled. She managed to regain her balance although she shot him a dirty look of irritation. If Cade noticed, he did not respond.

Lemuel interrupted now. He looked into her eyes, drawing her attention away from Cade. "Girl, I have to get the bullet out or else he'll get lead poisonin'. I'll have to cut it out."

"C-cut it out?" she stuttered. "But what if he should die?"

Lemuel nodded slowly. "There's a chance that he could have already lost too much blood, but I need to try either way." Seeing her open her mouth to retort, he spoke even more harshly. "Is that understood? If I do this he may survive. And if you want him to live through the operation, swallow your tears. Your blubberin' is gettin' on my nerves."

Elizabeth nodded, her eyes still swimming in tears. "All right." A thought occurred to her, and she tilted her head to meet his gaze. "Have you ever dealt with a bullet wound?"

Lemuel expelled a breath of irritation. "I've seen worse. But this man has come too far to be left to die. I'm aimin' to get him back to his health. If you're the prayin' type then you best send up a petition to God. Your husband is gonna need all the help he can get."

Lemuel's urgent tone of voice brought more tears. "Yes, sir, I-I do. I will pray to Him."

The elderly Canadian nodded shortly. Turning to Cade standing behind him, Lemuel changed the subject abruptly as he always seemed to do. "And I'll be a needin' your help too, boy. The Lord ain't goin' to raise the man from his sick bed without a little elbow grease now, is he?"

Elizabeth watched Cade's reaction. The outlaw stared at Lemuel. His expression seemed almost puzzled by the old man's interest in helping David. After a long moment, he shrugged. "I guess we can set up camp here for tonight. We'll leave at dawn tomorrow."

———

A day later

The voice was low and rumbly, interrupting her deep sleep. Her lashes fluttered against pale cheeks before she stirred and opened her eyes. Seeing a husky form leaning slightly over her, she sat up straight in the uncomfortable makeshift bed and stared up into Lemuel Ellis Keagan's eyes.

"Wh-where am I?" she stuttered, looking around herself in confusion.

The elderly man tipped his head in acknowledgement. "At the hideout," he answered.

The girl frowned. "Hideout?"

"Where the Addison brothers are stayin'."

She grimaced. "Oh, so where they count their money after stealing? I suppose that means I am in a den of thieves," she muttered partially to herself. Then, "Wh-what is wrong?" she asked, anxiety written all over her face after hearing the eerie silence. She looked intently up into the tall Canadian's gray eyes and felt a flood of terror surge through her soul. What if David were dead?

Hearing footstep, she turned around to see Casey standing behind Lemuel. She forced a smile at the boy to which he returned. Then his expression transformed to pure misery. "Miss, I'm sorry about…"

She smiled wanly; sadly, apparently already resigned. Through the haze of sadness, she felt surprised that she was taking his death so well. "His name was David Harrison, Casey."

He nodded. "Yes, him."

She slouched her shoulders dejectedly. "Going to another world…leaving me behind…" She mused aloud.

He mistook her meaning and thought that she meant him and his brothers. "Yes, ma'am. That is what I came to tell you."

His eyes were downcast and instantly she knew. "You don't have to tell me. I already knew he was dead." She spoke the words bitterly.

He stared at her in puzzlement. "But I ain't dead, and neither is Cade or Calder!"

Now it was her turn to frown. "I beg your pardon?"

"Cade says we are leavin' the territory today." He looked into her eyes. "But I don't want to go."

She eyed him, confused. "Whatever are you talking about, Casey?"

He bit his lip. "I'm sayin' that Cade wants us to go away from here."

He looked so disheartened that she felt her heart reach out to him even though she still hadn't a clue what he meant or was talking about. "Who is 'we'?" she questioned, her green eyes probing into his soul.

"Cade, me, and Calder. Cade mentioned that he hopes we'll run into Cass, Cole, Cody, and Connor. But I doubt it because they are down south in...in..." He paused, squinting. "I think it's a country called...A-mer-i-ca." He spelled out the word slowly, trying to remember how he had heard his older brothers pronounced it. "But we gotta leave 'cause Cade says we gotta find a new area to be..." He shifted one foot slightly. "To be what we are. You know what I mean?" He looked at her intently.

She nodded. Oh yes, she understood exactly what the boy meant. It was obvious. That rotten snake Cade Addison. That rude, ill-mannered lout intended to hightail it out of the North West Territories with his little brothers in tow.

Controlling bigot.

Anger sparked into her soul once more.

The boy was still talking. "And I don't want to go!"

She was relieved to hear that at least. "You don't want to go?"

The boy nodded his head. "No, ma'am. I mean, *yes*, ma'am! I want to stay here with you. Can I?"

Elizabeth was surprised. She fumbled for the right words to say. "I would really like you to stay here with me, but you can't." The boy's hopeful expression clouded in dismay. She hurried on. "This is not my decision. It is just that since David is…" She faltered. "Well, since David is no longer here on earth with us, I just will not be able to provide for you." Elizabeth tried to swallow the lump in her throat. How she hated herself for speaking in such a phlegmatic comportment. Even though she abhorred the thought of having Cade Addison take care of him, she knew the outlaw was much better qualified than she. After all, he knew how to survive in this wild land of Canada.

And she had no idea.

Chapter Twenty Two

Cade and Calder opened the small door and entered the cabin. They had just finished saddling their horses. Upon hearing voices in the other room, they ambled up to the door. Seeing his youngest brother sitting next to that fool redheaded girl, Cade felt irritation rekindle within his soul.

"Alert, what are you doin'?" he bellowed. "I feel mighty anxious to give you a lickin'. Quit that idle slackin' and get to packin' up the supplies! We're leavin' in a few minutes."

The young boy flinched at his eldest brother's strident tone. He straightened and was about to leap to his feet when he felt the beautiful red-haired angel stiffen beside him.

"How dare you." Her voice began at a low whisper but then raised up into a higher octave and then higher still. "How dare you!"

"What was that?" Cade's eyes seemed to pierce directly through her.

She glared at him and then got off the bed, although slowly and purposely. She did not speak another word for a few moments. She and Cade had themselves a stare down, glaring vehemently. Of course, wasn't it just like him to win? She felt her eyes sting and before she could stop it, she blinked. Glaring across the small room at Cade, she saw that he hadn't even blinked once. He continued to stare at her. Unwavering. Proud.

Like the pompous outlaw he was.

"You got somethin' to say, little miss, then say it!"

171

The voice jarred on her nerves. "Yes, I most certainly do."

That snake of an outlaw's partially amused expression was positively maddening. "Then say it. Come on, I ain't got all day!"

"What I want to say is that you are a…" She paused, considering the thoughts she wished more than anything to put into words. Very familiar feelings of spite and hate surged throughout her. She spit them out, not thinking about the consequences. "You are a rude, ill mannered, shallow-brained man. You are an undiplomatic outlaw and a pompous idiot!"

The girl fought a triumphant smirk while he cocked a brow. Upon seeing Casey's adoring expression, she felt a surge of protectiveness flood through her. She wanted to cry, "You don't have to go with your renegade brothers! I changed my mind; you may stay with me after all." But then came reality. Harsh, cruel reality. It beat down at the door of her heart, the rage of hatred and vengeance shattering the dream.

God had it in His heart to end her life very soon. What was she even thinking? No matter how appealing that thought may sound to her, she had to ground her selfish desires away from it. God would probably not hesitate to kill her even if Casey were with her. No, she would stay far away from the boy. He had his whole life ahead of him; she would not be a part of his murder.

A cough brought her mind to the present. Elizabeth held her breath, fear smiting her heart. What had she just done? Cade Addison already hated her so what had prompted her to discard the truce they had uttered only a day ago?

Tears welled up in her eyes. She resorted to the last option on her mind to do.

To beg and implore for mercy.

She sank down to her knees in front of Cade Addison, tears now flowing freely. "I am desperately sorry," she sobbed. "But it was an accident!" She clasped her hands together a mere inch below her chin. "Please…can't you reconsider? Can't you forgive me for what I said? Give me any punishment you deem appropriate for my actions but don't kill me, I beg of you!" Closing her eyes and drawing a deep breath, she lowered her head.

Cade Addison shook his head at the scene at his feet. The situation struck him as entirely amusing, and he felt his surprise almost dissolve into a smile.

Almost, but not quite.

He straightened his shoulders. Pasting on a gruff expression, he narrowed his eyes and tapped his foot in front of her. Startled, she opened her eyes and looked down at his boot with stupefied features before she finally gathered enough courage to lift her head.

"Get up, will you." Cade spoke a little harshly, but Lemuel read laughter in it.

After gawking at him a moment longer, she hastily got to her feet. He did not move one finger to help her up as David had done. He simply regarded her overtly. She dug her fingers in her sweaty palms.

The outlaw surveyed her for a long moment. "Before I decide, I will say what I think of you." He paused. "You are a ninny, an airhead, addlebrained, addlepated fool." He duplicated what she had said about him. "And you are an undiplomatic female. A pompous idiot!" He offered her an ironic smile. "And now you may go, although I ain't quite sure why you'd want to leave without your husband anyways."

Elizabeth stiffened. Her anger flared once more. She would go, all right, but not until she gave him a piece of her mind. She straightened indignantly. "And you, *sir*, are a slothful, shiftless and delinquent outlaw!"

Cade's eyes narrowed. "Is that right?" he questioned slowly.

She nodded furiously. "Yes."

He raised an eyebrow. "Do you mean all them things you're sayin'?"

She frowned slightly. What did he mean by that? Momentarily startled, she answered hesitantly. "Y-yes, I do," she squeaked. It was then that she apparently realized she was making things worse for herself by her continuous talking. She cleared her throat. "I I mean no…I don't. Of course I don't!"

"You do mean them, don't you?" He eyed her suspiciously.

She shook her head fast. "No, I really don't."

"You're lyin'. I know you are."

She knew her game was up. He could see right through her that she did, indeed, mean every word concerning him. "All right," she said dejectedly. "I admit I am lying. I do mean everything I just said because they are true." Her voice lowered because there was a lump so big it nearly filled her throat. "You aren't happy with who you are, are you? You are not happy with the fact that you are an outlaw. Deep down in your heart, I am sure you wish you could become something everyone would respect. If only you would *change!* Why don't you, Cade?!"

He was surprised as her voice transformed from hate into urgency. Why was she making him feel squeamish? This girl was getting on his nerves. She was edging him to voice the terrifying, paralyzing truth that Cade Addison wanted his brothers to look up to him as a man who could do anything he wanted to do. He just wanted respect.

His brothers obeyed him; oh yes, they eyed him with a half respect, half terror. To them he was the chief of their life. What they didn't realize was that Cade Addison was a man uncertain of both life and death. Outwardly, he tried to be tough and brave. But inwardly he was a coward.

He licked his lips. Exchanging a brief glance with Lemuel Ellis Keagan, the proud outlaw spoke the words in an almost trembling voice. "Because I can't. This is my life!"

"No, Cade!" She swallowed away a lump in her throat. "Each single person in the world has his own path to take. There are two paths. One for evil, the other for good. You chose the path of being an outlaw. You became a man feared by many…" Her voice broke. Tears spilled over her cheeks. "You're the only one who can change yourself. If only you would *try.*" Swiping away tears, she drew her hand out and shakily took his in hers. He stared down stupidly, not saying one word. "I will pray for you," she continued softly. "I am very sure there is a God and although He hates me, I will pray for Him to show you that you can become someone respectable and no longer a murderer."

Her words touched too close to home.

He whirled around and after barking a curt order to both Calder and Casey to follow him, he stalked out the cabin door towards their horses that patiently waited, swinging himself up onto his mount. Cade was shaking both inwardly and shaking outwardly. Elizabeth Davison's words had touched a soft cord within his hardened, embittered soul. And he really was afraid.

Inside the cabin everything was a deathly silence. Calder grabbed his saddlebag and left the cabin. Elizabeth glanced at the boy near her side. He was desperately attempting to remain calm, but she saw he was near tears.

"Casey," she choked out, her voice congested with emotion. "You must go with your brother."

He began to shake his head. "No, I want to stay here with you!"

She nodded, tears of anguish spilling over pale cheeks. "I want that too, but it won't happen as your brother will not permit it. Cade is your elder brother; you must follow his commands."

The nine year old was barely holding back his tears of disappointment. "No, I can't go. I just can't leave you!"

"You must."

Her voice was firm yet filled with love and softness. Looking into her beautiful eyes, he knew that she was right. He bit his lip to hold back the tears. "I will come back to you. I promise."

Tears trickled down her cheeks. "Please do not think I don't love you. It is quite the opposite, really. In fact I love you so much that I am telling you to *go* with Cade and Calder. You are Casey Addison.

You must grow up to be a good, honest man. Do not be poisoned by all the death and fighting you have witnessed in your young life. Remain who you are now and be as pure and innocent as possible."

"Do you...do you really mean it, miss?" he breathed, eyes wide with wonder.

She nodded. "Of course I mean every word I am speaking! I love you with all of my heart and soul."

He threw himself into her arms, latching his hands around her neck. "Don't make me go," he begged, a lone tear falling. "Please let me stay here with you always."

"Oh, Casey." Her words ended in a strangled sob. "Don't make this parting any harder than it already is. Please."

His grip tightened. "Don't make me go with *him*. Oh, please let me stay. I don't love him like you!" The words burst out before he could stop them.

Elizabeth's eyes widened. "Do you really mean that? Do you really love me?"

"Love you?" he breathed. "Love you? Oh, miss, I've loved you since I first saw you! You are a heavenly red headed angel that has come swoopin' down from Heaven to help us all, ain't you?"

She couldn't help but laugh through her tears. "You are sweet, but that hardly describes me."

"Don't you see who you really are? You're an angel!"

Elizabeth couldn't have been more surprised. The boy was calling her an angel? She suppressed a smile. Utterly ridiculous. If she were an angel, most assuredly she would be like one of Lucifer's.

"I will never forget you; I promise you that. You will forever be instilled upon my mind and memory."

He swiped at a tear, determined to be brave. "But what if I never see you again?"

She thought a moment before responding. "Our life's road has many bends in it. It does not go on forever in a long, straight line. It has corners that we have yet to round and see what is in store for us. For now it seems that there is another bend here. You must go with your brothers; I must go my own way. Perhaps there is another bend in our futures that will allow us to reunite. We must always try to look on the bright side of things, do you not agree?"

He nodded glumly. "I suppose so, but I still don't think it is fair that I gotta go with Cade."

She drew him into a warm hug. "I love you. Behave yourself. Do not do anything that may aggrieve Cade or Calder."

He squirmed out of her embrace. "I wish they wasn't my brothers," he mumbled.

"Casey," she reproached. "You ought to be grateful to have brothers! I have no one at all anymore."

The boy blanched at her sharp words. "I…I'm sorry."

She closed her eyes. "No, it is I who ought to apologize. I am getting too tense now."

In reality, she was hanging on by one last thread of endurance. If she didn't have any stamina, she would have burst into floods of tears a long time ago. Instead, she gripped the last few threads of the remaining forbearance and attempted a smile. She must be brave… at least for Casey's sake.

Elizabeth choked on tears. David was dead. She had not a place to stay. She had not an ounce of comprehension how to survive in this wild and vast land. She drew a breath to better steady her nerves. "I wish it were all different. But it is not. We *must* face reality."

He nodded his head in forlorn subjection to her words. "Yes, miss."

The cabin door creaked open once more as Calder re-entered.

She gathered Casey close within her embrace one last time. Resting her chin upon his soft hair, she wished this moment would never end. She wanted to never let him go.

His arms tightened about her. She swallowed away another choking lump within her throat. Finally, she eased back. He did not. He clung to her as though she was his only savior.

"Casey," she croaked. "You mustn't keep your brother waiting."

Slowly he drew back and gazed into her eyes. "You won't ever know how much I love you, miss. You are an angel of light within a storm of darkness." After one more endearing look her way as though to place her image in his thoughts forever, he then turned and ran out the door towards his eldest brother before she could see the stream of tears that were falling. She went and stood by the small window, watching him go, crying silently.

"Miss."

She turned. It was Calder.

The boy self-consciously bit his lip, keeping his eyes trained on the ground. "I…uh…just wanted to say that I'm sorry the way things turned out." He swallowed hard. "I wish I wish Cade…" His voice trailed off.

She nodded, understanding he also wished Cade were kinder and that their life was different. "So do I," she murmured.

As if drawn by an unexplainable force, he jerked his head towards her and met her eyes. "I am also sorry I had to…" He drew a breath. "I'm sorry I had to hold that gun on you, miss. You ain't never deserved the treatment Cade ordered me to give you."

It was unspoken yet Elizabeth understood. The boy was attempting to apologize in a roundabout way for the outlaw lifestyle. She took his hand and he looked startled, but Elizabeth did not appear aware of his discomfort. "I shall pray for each of you." Her voice broke. "I will pray that God will keep you all safe, and that your brother will change." She swiped at her tears, angry she could not control her emotions. After all, if the men could then so could she.

Calder swallowed. "I…I hope we can come back here again sometime. Not as outlaws, but as honest men."

She smiled at him through her the glistening tears. "I will pray for that too."

He offered a tentative smile before the loud, grating voice of Cade broke the silence. "Calder, we gotta get goin'! Get over here."

The boy jumped. "I-I need to go."

She nodded, maintaining her brave facade. "I shall see you all again someday. I am sure of that fact."

He ducked his head slightly. She could see he didn't believe her. "Yes, miss. Goodbye."

She began to cry once again.

So much for her withstanding exterior.

Elizabeth watched Calder swing a leg over his chestnut mount in a quick, fluid motion. As the tears cascaded down her cheeks, she watched them vacate the premises. Before she lost sight of them, however, both Casey and Calder twisted themselves around in the saddle and waved farewell. Her heart leapt with joy, and she returned their gist of friendship.

I do not understand, she cried silently, watching their retreat. *Why is this happening? What is going to happen to me?*

Chapter Twenty Three

A week later

God, I know it's been a long time since we've talked. I'm sorry I've been so obstinate in my former years. I am here askin' You to forgive me for how stupid I acted. I was a fool, Lord. A complete fool. You are probably fed up with me, and maybe I'm already crossed out of Your Book of Life. If I am still in it, though, I'd like to ask forgiveness for my sins. I-I know I don't deserve no forgiveness. I know I ain't deservin' of Your time. Yet I am still askin' You if You'd forgive me and all my sins. Please, Lord?

Peace instilled upon the old man's mind as he remembered Jesus' sacrifice and the promise of salvation to any who ask. His heart was free from the bonds of Satan. He was free from his past. He was free from the burden that had been upon his back for all of his life.

Love found its way into his heart and soul. Love and peace from God above. Lemuel Ellis Keagan praised the Lord God to the ends of the earth for His merciful kindness and goodwill to sinful man. *Thank You!* he whispered reverently. *Thank You.*

———

Even after the Addison brothers had left, Lemuel had stayed to look after that fool girl and her husband. He was fearful she might neglect to take care of herself as his Olivia had done. As strange as he thought she was, he didn't want that to happen to even her.

Elizabeth was so distraught that despite Lemuel's averment that David wasn't dead yet, she had refused to go into the other room. She didn't even know how her husband was doing.

Now he watched the young girl across the room. Tears trickled down her freckled cheeks. "Girl," he began, but the girl jumped up and whirled to face him.

"Who are you?" she demanded before seeing his face. Then she relaxed, relief filling her tone. "It is only you."

He nodded shortly. "Yes."

Suddenly, she jumped up and ran across the room into his arms, her tears instantly dampening his rough coat. She cried aloud, sobs filled with desperation.

As for Lemuel, he was stunned. He hadn't had a child seek him as a solid stone of protection and reassurance since his Olivia had been a little girl. And this wasn't even his daughter!

"What is going on? Why are you crying?"

————

Elizabeth heard the footsteps behind them and she uttered a piercing shriek before whirling around. She clutched Lemuel's arm in sheer terror. *Oh, Lord, is it a ghost?* With shock, she found herself face-to-face with non-other but David Harrison. He seemed still slightly unsteady upon his feet for he swayed a moment before leaning a shoulder against the doorframe. His broad shoulders and imposing height seemed to take up most of the space in the cabin.

The corners of his lips tugged up into an impish grin. "Crying again? When are you going to learn that tears do not solve every problem in life?"

He was teasing; she knew that. For probably the first time in her life, Elizabeth didn't know what to do. She simply stared at him, transfixed in shock. And then something snapped within her. Somehow she managed to find her voice, and a sob broke free from numb lips. "David, is that really you or am I imagining it?"

The tall man took her hands and laughed softly. "Who else do you think it would be?"

She burst into tears. He frowned, puzzled. "Now what did I say wrong?"

Choking on sobs, she just managed to utter words that were scarcely legible. "I thought…"

"You thought what?"

She drew a breath. "I thought you were dead, David," she admitted.

He grinned then. "Dead? Apparently it wasn't my time to be taken by the good Lord."

A clearing of the throat behind her reminded her of the old man's presence. She turned to see the tall woodsman leaning against the wall, observing them calmly.

David looked up and, espying the man who had saved his life, nodded at Lemuel. His eyes turned back to Elizabeth. "I best thank him."

She looked surprised. "Thank him for what?"

His eyebrows shot up. "Not thank him for saving my life?" He shook his head, attempting to look stern. "Where are your manners?"

She blinked. "I-I never thought to thank him. I was just so disheartened with everything that had occurred I suppose I did not realize his presence." She hesitated, biting her lip. "He didn't…he didn't take care of you, did he?"

He cocked his head impishly. "Of course he did. Would I be alive if he hadn't? I suggest you also assist me in thanking him. Don't you agree?"

"Y-yes, of course." She nodded almost stupidly for she was yet in a daze.

————

Lemuel Ellis Keagan watched them draw nearer to him. The shock at seeing the tall young man suddenly on his feet and looking so well, when all this time for the past week Lemuel had expected him to die, was astounding. Yet he knew it was a miracle. How else could any man become well enough to walk in one week and move without obvious pain?

David reached Lemuel and instantly extended his hand. The elderly man stared at the outstretched token of gratitude. Something Lemuel Ellis Keagan was not very accustomed to.

"I want to thank you for saving my life and for taking care of Beth. I surely would have died without your considerate care."

"Weren't no problem. No doubt you'd have done the same."

David nodded. "Nonetheless, I thank you."

The elderly Canadian shifted one foot. "I ain't good with thank you's and that type of thing, but in this case I suppose it won't hurt for me to say thank *you*."

Elizabeth's mouth dropped. David frowned, puzzled. "I'm afraid I don't understand what you mean."

"What I mean is that you have both shown me somethin' that I ain't never really thought about before. You have taught me that I still have an opportunity to change into a better man." He looked down into Elizabeth's wide eyes as he spoke the words. She knew then that he must have overheard what she'd said to Cade Addison.

Lemuel Ellis Keagan met David's eyes once again. "I'm thinkin' that I want to go with you both to your new land and help get you started." He looked slightly awkward. "That is, if you can put it past you that I was an outlaw."

He had said *was*. Elizabeth's smile widened. She grasped the man's sun-tanned, work-ladened hand into hers. "Of course we can!" she exclaimed, euphoria bubbling within her. Glancing up at David, she sobered slightly. "At least *I* can." In other words, the tall man swiftly realized, it was David's decision.

He nodded his consent. "I can forget your past as long as you won't ever go back into it."

Keagan's solemn expression and answer blew away any doubts

the two young people may have entertained. "I can promise you that."

She beamed at David and then at the now changed man.

Lemuel Ellis Keagan was becoming a man she was proud to know.

———

Three days later

David could not believe the change in Elizabeth. The girl had transformed from her obstinate, arrogant attitude and now actually listened to him! The Lord Almighty had altered her heart into a person so beautiful that her loveliness now shone from within her and combined with her outer beauty. An expression that portrayed pure beauty because she was now free from her former bitterness and anger. She had grown to realize that God did love and care for her. She now believed in His existence.

David knew Elizabeth had always attempted to look to other things in life that could be her savior. But now she had One. The best One anyone could ever have. She was no longer an orphan. She had been adopted by her heavenly Father who had promised never to forsake her.

David Harrison inwardly prayed for her in the difficult life ahead of them. He half knew what to expect. Elizabeth? No, she thought that their new land would be filled with flowers and honey. Poetry and songs. What she didn't realize was that there would be times where they would no doubt wish to be back in manicured, prestigious England. Questioning God in times of peril or unease, there would be trials ahead like they had never before experienced. But, David reminded himself, they had God on their side. And with Him, all things are possible.

Including moving mountains.

Elizabeth couldn't help but smile. Her heart felt so alive. There was so much joy inside both her heart and soul.

We are almost home. She blinked away a tear. *Why am I crying about that?* she wondered. *Perhaps because we have nearly reached the end of our long journey? Because I have captured a glimpse of the rainbow? Or is it just because I feel such peace and contentedness filling my heart because I am so loved by Him?*

She inhaled-exhaled in quick succession, silently offering up a prayer to the greatest Redeemer of all time.

Thank You, Lord, for everything You've ever done for me. You have welcomed me to inherit the Kingdom of the most High. Please protect Casey and Calder. And Cade…

Lord, I am sure that man deserves the biggest tongue-lashing ever, but when I think about myself…well, really, I wasn't any better than him. I was every bit as abominable as him, if not worse. David told me that in John 14:6, You said, "I am the way, the truth, and the life: no man cometh unto the Father, but by me." I know I am unworthy to even tie Your shoelaces, but thank You for dying upon the cross so that I might be cleansed through Your precious blood.

Help me keep my temper in check and help keep my mouth shut from saying things that are foolish. Watch over us all, Lord. Help us. Protect us. We really need You now…probably more than ever before.

From this moment onward, I shall strive to be Your faithful servant forever. I remain Yours truly. Elizabeth Davison.

Lemuel Ellis Keagan regarded the rolling hills and majestic mountains, inhaling the fresh scent of pine. The bees played hide and seek with the flowers as they buzzed from one to another. But his mind was on distant things. Things that involved that fool girl and tall man.

He wanted to help them; teach them. Fill their minds with

details about how to live in this country and how to provide food for themselves. He wanted to teach them all he knew about life. He wanted his knowledge to be passed down to them and possibly the next generation.

Unfortunately, the addlepated girl had probably never known a day in her life of affliction and adversity, though. He guessed she had most likely owned a life of ease and prosperity. But how would she take it when she finally realized that she would have to work in order to survive?

The old man prayed for the Lord's help in the journey ahead of them. These two young people thought the journey to the North West Territories was hard enough. What they didn't realize was that when they finally reached their new land, their journey would just be beginning!

God, my only prayer is that You keep that filly's mouth shut. Maybe then I can think more rationally. She's gonna make me a grave before my time has come.

Chapter Twenty Four

Lemuel spoke, stemming the stream of words that spilled from Elizabeth's lips.

"Well, are you folks ready to see your land?"

Elizabeth's expression brightened like a glowing lantern. Her excitement was obvious. "Yes!" she squeaked. "I'm more ready than I've ever been before in all my life."

David managed to maintain his composed facial features and merely nodded.

Lemuel Ellis Keagan dismounted; David and Elizabeth did likewise. As she gazed about herself, words still tumbling from her lips, she suddenly gasped. The sight that met the girl's eyes left her unduly shaken. And as she slowly looked up at David, tears sprang to her eyes. What place had David brought her too? A place occupied with the same wild underbrush they had passed for most of the ride. It was a land requiring hard labor to make it a presentable home and a land that would bring her nothing but sorrow after sorrow.

It seemed David knew exactly what she was thinking.

"I know that this is not what you were expecting. Quite frankly, I admit I also was expecting some buildings and evidence of true habitation." His voice trailed off as she continued to stare ahead, tears pooling in her eyes before silently streaming down her cheeks. Her previous euphoria was now wiped off her face. David's heart was so heavy for her it could have sunk to the depths of the ocean like a rock.

Poor Elizabeth was devastated. She had expected so much and, to her way of thinking, was receiving so little. Her expectations had apparently been over-imagined, for David could almost feel the disappointment radiating off her in waves. She had dramatized their new land to the extent that it had appeared as an ivory tower. How wrong she had been. How disappointed she now was. And that was all because she had expected too much.

He was surprised that she hadn't erupted in a wailing, blubbering mess of hysterics yet.

"Why?" she whispered, a tear snaking down her cheek only to hit her chin. "Why?"

"Elizabeth."

The girl's head tilted up. She moistened her parched lips. "Wh-what?" she stammered, swallowing the lump in her throat. "Did you just call me...?" The dam broke, just as he had suspected it would. She burst into a flood of tears. "David," she sniffed. "You have never before called me by my full name. Why did you do it just now?"

He considered her question thoroughly before responding. "It may sound childish and prejudice, but it was because your name reminded me of my aunt. During our journey north, however, I came to realize that I was wrong. Aunt Elizabeth was a genteel aunt, and when she passed away from scarlet fever..." He hesitated. "I am reluctant to say this but I foolishly blamed and resented you for something that I now know is ridiculous. I witlessly begrudged you because you reminded me of her. I now know I was a fool. Can you forgive me for my injudicious acrimony?"

The girl bit her lip, another flood of tears restocking themselves. Peacefulness swelled within her heart. "Thank you," she said softly, her heart filled with happiness she had never before experienced. "Of course I forgive you. And please permit me to also offer an apology for my vengeful malice towards you in most of the previous years."

David grinned. "Are we now friends?" he asked. "Or are you going to persist upon being enemies all our days?"

The girl smiled up him. "I would very much like to terminate our rift and become friends with you."

"Then from this moment onwards, you and I will forget our revengeful past and focus on our future. We will live and toil in this land as friends together creating our new life."

Elizabeth sniffed away her tears at his words. And it was then that for the first time in her entire life, she felt blessed. She felt immense thankfulness to her Savior for bringing her to this land. The girl gazed up into his eyes, her heart soaring with floored surprise. This year would bring tears and laughter, sorrow and happiness. Throughout it all, however, Elizabeth hoped it would be a year filled with adventure. Adventures that would become memories in her future to think back upon when she was old and gray.

Their long journey certainly had turned out different than they'd all anticipated, but it was her new beginning. She determined to make this land her home. After all, the good Lord was with her.

A smile curved her lips. Inwardly and outwardly she had everything she could ever want. She had David as her friend and guardian, and she had Jesus to watch over and guide her. She had contentment and peace, joy and thanksgiving. She was whole and alive.

The fiery redhead turned to glance up at the tall man who stood by her side. He smiled down at her. "How do you like your glimpse of the rainbow?" he asked.

Flashing him a dazzling smile, she squared her slender shoulders. "It was smaller than I expected it to be," she admitted honestly. "I initially expected there to a brilliant, glorious rainbow that stretched forth across the firmament, showering me with gold. However, I can now see that without doing our share of the work, there will not be any reward. It will be hard work to cultivate our new life but I am positive that with a profusion of prayer and determination, we will succeed in our dream and build a home."

He laughed. "I can't believe you just said that, Beth. Who would have known that you would obtain such remarkable calculations?"

She stiffened. "Are you mocking me?"

"No, no, of course not. I am merely playing sarcasm."

He chuckled at her scrunched expression of disgruntled frustration. "Why must you tease me?" she scowled.

"Why must you be so gullible?" he returned, chuckling.

Elizabeth tilted her head back to meet David's gaze. "I am *not* gullible!" she protested. "You just…just seem to have a way about you that makes me confused."

He tousled her hair affectionately. "I don't believe it." His voice dropped two octaves. "Are you really finally implying that I am more clever than you?"

She slapped his arm, frowning. "Certainly not," she retorted. "I-I merely meant…"

"Come now, it isn't necessary to object to the facts and challenge them in a most childish display of a temper," he admonished.

She jutted out her lower lip, sulking. "Why are you always such an infernal exasperation?"

He grinned. "Maybe because you don't seem to realize who triggers my 'infernal exasperation' button."

With a partially aggravated throw up of her hands, the girl craned her neck to the sky. "This is our new home," she murmured. "The home we've ventured thousands of miles to see. The land where we are going to live."

David rested a hand on her shoulder. She shrugged it off. "Don't patronize me," she snapped. "I am still upset with you."

"I wasn't patronizing, Beth," he explained. "I was merely offering you the comfort that I will always be here with you on our new land."

She gave a rather unladylike snort. "Oh, that is such a comfort."

Pure sarcasm, he thought. She had finally learned how to use it appropriately. A grin twitched his lips. Elizabeth. This was Elizabeth. The sassy, fiery, impulsive girl that was like his little sister. The little girl he'd always known had changed. God had changed her. He had softened her embittered heart because He had offered her a free gift that paved way to an eternity in glory with Him. She had accepted it with joy and thanksgiving. She was no longer an orphan. She was the daughter of the King of Kings!

She turned around to meet his gaze and smirked. "Shocked?"

He smiled at her. "Yes. You've changed, Beth."

She flipped her red head. "Your point?"

"That *is* my point. You've changed."

Rolling her eyes, her tinkling laugh swept across the plane. "That's it, though? You still haven't determined whether I've changed for good or bad."

His eyes softened. "Good. Definitely good."

A smile curved her mouth. "Are you insinuating I was *bad* before?"

He shrugged. "And if you were?"

"I'd completely agree."

His mouth dropped at the seriousness in her tone. This was not the old Elizabeth. The old Elizabeth would have never admitted she was wrong. The old Elizabeth would have never admitted that she was not always such a nice person. The old Elizabeth was proud in a high-minded, self-centered way.

"What?"

"I said I'd completely agree. I was a self-centered girl."

He blinked. "I confess I was not expecting you to admit that…"

With a mischievous wink and flashing grin, she made a face that was best left undescribed. It bore a striking resemblance to… He frowned. Was she teasing? He hadn't even been aware she had the *ability* to tease!

"As you've said, I've changed. Or more appropriately, God changed me." Her tone sobered. "You were right, David, although I refused to acknowledge it. God's ways are higher than our ways but He always looks out for our good. He allowed all that recently transpired for a reason." She turned to meet his gaze, and her eyes glistened with tears. "Thank you for being patient with me," she whispered. "Thank you…for everything. Your words, your decisions, your assistance, your respect, and for being the big brother I never had. Even if I *am* yet under your care." Although her chin trembled with a strong resolve to not burst into tears, she managed a tremulous smile.

"It's a rather strange situation, isn't it?" he replied softly. "We are friends, yet according to the law you are technically still under my guardianship." He hesitated. "Do you think you can withstand the remaining years, even in name only?"

She nodded. "It's all right. I also overreacted regarding the indenture." A dazzling smile flashed up at him, revealing straight, pearly teeth. "You have behaved gallantly, treating me with respect. As gallantly as a knight in shining armor thundering across the pasture upon his white steed to save a young damsel in distress."

"I behaved gallantly?" His rumbling laugh was like a rock slide. "You're calling me gallant? How the tables have turned."

She blushed. "Well, I admit I also overreacted regarding my fantasy. You were right. It *was* a fantasy. And I've now come to the conclusion that I don't require a knight in shining armor. I'm perfectly capable of looking after myself."

"Ahem."

David and Elizabeth turned to meet Lemuel's rather bored expression. "Done talkin' yet?" he growled. "I'm about bored to tears hearin' you both jabber about knights and shinin' armor."

Elizabeth opened her mouth to retort, but David touched her arm in a warning. She acquiesced...

And changed her original intention to snap at him by replacing it with a slightly artificial twist.

"You're a good man, Mr. Keagan. Thank you for helping me."

He snorted. "Even though I lied, murdered, stole, and was a despicable outlaw? Even though I was cruel, hateful and wicked?"

A flush formed on her cheekbones. She swallowed to hide her growing embarrassment. "Well, I-I suppose I overreacted."

"Seems you've been doin' a lot of that, then," he grumbled.

She stiffened, but David elbowed her to maintain her frustration.

"I'm sorry." It had taken a profusion of courage to voice the words. Pride swept through her. She'd really done it. She'd admitted her erroneous ways. That was a hard fall for her dignity.

Lemuel eyed her before guffawing. "That's it?" he bellowed. " 'I'm sorry'? That's the extent of your apology for what I all had to go through? After hearin' your high-pitched, squeakin' mouse voice, your shrieks of fear, and your constant jabberin' so that my ears are practically numb and deaf, all I get in return is a mere 'I'm sorry'?"

Her jaw dropped. What a ridiculously self-centered man! How dare he ask for more of an apology? She hadn't needed to make amends, but she had a kind heart. The ignorant bloke expected more? The only 'more' he'd be getting would be a good punch in the nose.

She drew back her fist, but David caught her arms before she could fulfill her intention. He laughed nervously as she struggled to escape his grip.

"Let me go!" she shouted. "He degraded my dignity again!"

David flashed Lemuel an uncertain smile. "She's still learning not to use force in an effort to get the desired result." He grunted as she stomped on his foot. An elbow jabbed his chest. She twisted and squirmed, fighting with a vigor of determination.

"Let me go!" she shrieked again. "I won't punch anyone after all. Just release me!"

———

Lemuel hid a grin.

It seemed the fool girl's 'husband' knew how to administer the appropriate reactions to her behavior. Had she actually punched him, Lemuel would have thrown her clean into the sky. She wouldn't know what had occurred until she'd come tumbling down and hit the ground with a hard *thud*. David had saved her skin again although Lemuel was sure that the birdbrained female really hadn't any indication that if it hadn't been for David, she would have met her Maker a long time ago. He was sure that she wouldn't have the ability to discern the difference between skunks and house cats; neither would the ninny have the capability to track a bed-wagon through a bog hole. Her brain cavity wouldn't make a drinking cup for a canary.

"Girl, stop your screechin' and hollerin'." The old man knit his brows. "I ain't never intended to upset you. I just think it'd be nice to get a little more of an apology. I had to put up with a whole lot at your expense, you know."

She stopped struggling for a moment as she appeared to remember what had all occurred. Swallowing her pride, she bit her lower lip. "Fine. I am terribly sorry for inflicting so much pain on you, and I will strive to improve my impulsiveness."

He nodded in satisfaction. "That's more what I was lookin' for."

She made a face and wrinkled her nose. David slowly released her then, although she glared at him and huffed with frustration.

Lemuel leveled his grey eyes on the two before him. "I also gotta ask you somethin' that's been keepin' me confused for the past few days. You originally said you were married but I never thought you acted like you're wed. And just now I also heard you mention that you were indentured to this man and that you are both friends." He scratched his head. "Friends ain't exactly what makes a married couple."

David and Elizabeth exchanged frantic glances. Elizabeth opened her mouth first. David poked her so she shut it again. She shot him a glare although he ignored her.

"You are right," he stated calmly, much to Elizabeth's surprise. "We are not married. We merely grew up together in England as children at my father's estate."

Lemuel frowned. "Why pretend to be married now, then?" he queried.

"There are people who often like to believe the worst in others. Elizabeth and I traveling alone together would undoubtedly bring talk. Nasty talk. Even if it is not true. I am sure you understand what I'm saying."

Lemuel nodded in understanding. "I see your point. Ignorant folks like them would ruin her reputation with their dirty thoughts and big mouths."

Elizabeth tugged on David's sleeve. "Excuse me, I am not invisible," she snapped. "At least include me in the conversation when talking about me in front of me."

Lemuel scowled. "The conversation didn't necessarily concern your input, girl," he growled. "Like I've already told you, keep your mouth shut."

She gasped. "Mr. Keagan " But David interrupted her introduction to a long argument by spinning her around to look at their land.

And as Lemuel Ellis Keagan looked at the two young people before him, a smile quirked his lips. The girl had spunk. She was feisty, fiery, strong, and determined. Of course she was stupid. In fact she was so stupid that Lemuel wondered if she could teach a hen to cluck. However, she would learn through her mistakes. He just hoped she didn't make so many mistakes that she would end her life before her appointed time.

He inhaled the scent of pines and poplars as his thoughts drifted towards life itself. The wilderness may be his earthly home, but his heavenly home was with his Lord Jesus Christ. He may have committed many mistakes and wrong choices, yet God had blotted them out. He was saved. Saved from damnation, saved from the world, saved from evil. Jesus had accepted him for who he was.

It was a beautiful day out. He was happy to be alive.

———

David Wesley Harrison and Elizabeth Hannah Davison scanned the expanse of land before them, each envisioning a tangible home that would one day no longer be just a dream.

They had seen a glimpse of the rainbow. Not literally, but figuratively. Throughout their journey north, she and David had overcome many obstacles. Yet they had continued onwards because their Lord had been with them every step of the way. When they shattered something in their own foolishness, He had helped them pick up the broken pieces. Without His miraculous ways, Elizabeth surmised that she would probably still be in England scrubbing floors and washing dishes, a dour expression upon her face. But He had found a way out. He had given her such joy. Oh, she knew she did not even have enough words to say in order to express her thankfulness and love to Him in appreciation for what He had done for her!

But God knew her heart. He knew she was nearly overflowing with joy. And all because of Him, she was now happy. Happy both internally and externally. All because Jesus was her King.

And now, Elizabeth concluded, came a silent promise of a better, brilliant beginning for their own ecstatic journey's ending.

Or so she thought...

Author's Note

At the beginning of *A Glimpse of the Rainbow,* Elizabeth Davison was a miserable indentured servant. She thought that there wasn't anything that could make her happy except prosperity. Instead of making use of the situation she was in, she became bitter and blamed God for life's heartaches. Alternately, at the beginning of this book, David Harrison, as the lord's son, was a boy without responsibility. But he was happy. There was neither bitterness nor anger within his heart.

Elizabeth disliked David Harrison *because* he was not bitter inside like she was. Gradually, a grudge of resentment evoked within her soul making her even more bitter than she already was towards life. She blamed God for everything bad that had transpired in her life and considered Him the doer of all evil things. As time passed, her resentment towards God only appeared to increase, making her even more spiteful. She concluded there was nothing to live for and that God was planning to murder her in a painful way. As if by some unexplainable cause, however, Elizabeth did not commit suicide as Satan himself suggested her to. She wanted to live, certain that there was a future of hope and peace out there somewhere.

Near the closing of their journey north, she finally becomes aware that the concord of a temporal world is unable to extinguish the yearning desire within her soul for something deeper and richer. God opened her eyes and revealed to her that He was indeed real. Despite how hard she strived to ignore His voice, she was unable to quench the burning aspiration within her soul to listen unto His words. And then believing on Him, she finally found true happiness.

Unfortunately, the girl gathered the impression that the rest of her life would be a 'happily ever after' Cinderella tale. She has yet to realize that life will go on with daily difficulties and struggles. With the Lord by her side, she will hopefully realize that she can resist and conquer all the temptations with Jesus' never ending help. But that is another story.

I am closing now. May bountiful blessings of promises rest upon each of you by our Lord and Savior, Jesus Christ.

For His Glory,

Philomena Van Oort